Rod Spro

ST ANTHONY'S FIRE

To Norma,
I hope you enjoy the tale,
it's all true.

Rod Sproon.
October 13th 2008.

Kings Hart Books

Published in 2008 by Kings Hart Books,
an imprint of Publishers UK Ltd
26 Beaumont Street Oxford, England OX1 2NP
01243 576016
www.kingshart.co.uk

Edited by Eileen O'Conor and Colin Shearing

The author has asserted his moral right to be identified as the author of this work.

A catalogue record for this book is available from the British Library.

The paper used in this book is from sustainable sources, certified by the Forest Stewardship Council.

ISBN 978-1-906154-10-3

To Andrea, with whom all is possible,
my lover, best friend, wife and mother to our fantastic children

✠

Think not that I am come to send peace on earth:
I came not to send peace, but a sword.
For I am come to set a man at variance against his father, and
the daughter against her mother, and the daughter in law
against her mother in law.
And a man's foes shall be they of his own household.
Matthew 10:34-36

PROLOGUE

The coach lurched, creaking over the rough surface of the road. Even the supple leather suspension had done little so far to relieve the elderly passenger from the rigours of the journey. His gnarled hand drew back the velvet curtain. Pope Urban II's rheumy eyes gazed bleakly out at the gray November countryside. The jolt from another pothole tore the heavy drape from his grasp, plunging the carriage once more into darkness.

The chill from the unheated carriage struck into his bones. He huddled down into his cloak trying to find some warmth. His address to the Council in a few days time would set in motion a train of events that was to last a thousand years; for it was here that Pope Urban II, God's Vicar on Earth and absolute ruler of The Holy Roman Catholic Church would issue his Papal Bull. He had come to the papacy as all popes had before him, determined not only to preserve the work of St Peter but to continue to build upon the rock of the Saint for the only true Faith on earth. He sighed in the darkness, his features grim. He ruled over a Europe seemingly at war with itself on an almost permanent basis, and he was tired of the in-fighting and political maneuverings that took up much of his and his Cardinals' time, tired of the never ending battle with the Italian kings over his rightful seat in Rome.

But now; he had received a letter from Constantinople; a letter that had burst upon his consciousness with the power of God's own voice. Within the darkness of the coach he prayed for divine inspiration to help him write a speech to be delivered in Clermont, a speech that would change the World forever.

"From the confines of Jerusalem and the city of Constantinople a horrible tale has gone forth and very frequently has been brought to our ears, namely that a race from the kingdom of the Persian, an accursed race, a race utterly alienated from God, has invaded the lands of the Christians and has put them to the sword. It has either razed the Churches of God to the ground, or desecrated them sacrilegiously using them to carry out their own pagan rites. They destroy the altars after having defiled them with their sacrifices. Every Christian man who is driven from his lands by these heathen and forced to forsake a house, or brethren, or sisters, or father, or mother, or wife, or children, or lands, in God's Name, shall be repaid a hundredfold and shall inherit everlasting life.

This land which you inhabit, shut in on all sides by the seas and surrounded by the mountain peaks, is too narrow for your large population; nor does it abound in wealth; and it furnishes scarcely food enough for its cultivators. Hence it is that you murder one another, that you wage war, and that frequently you perish by mutual wounds. Let therefore hatred depart from among you, let your quarrels end, let wars cease, and let all dissensions and controversies slumber.

Enter upon the road to the Holy Sepulchre; wrest that land from that wicked race, and subject it to yourselves. God has conferred upon you above all nations great glory in arms. Accordingly undertake this journey for the remission of your sins, with the assurance of the imperishable glory of the Kingdom of Heaven."

I, or rather the Lord, beseech you as Christ's heralds to publish this everywhere and to persuade all people of whatever rank, foot soldiers and knights, poor and rich, to carry aid promptly to those Christians and to destroy that vile race from the lands of our friends. I say this to those who are present, it is meant also for those who are absent. Moreover,God wills it."

<u>Council of Clermont, France. November 1095</u>

CHAPTER ONE

Acre, April 29th 1291

This was the end! After 200 years of unrelenting holy warfare the Infidels were finally driving the Crusader armies back into the sea.

Henri de Montfort was sitting on the breakwater eating figs when this realisation hit him. Shading his eyes from the sun glitter coming off the sea, he watched as yet another overloaded Pisan or Venetian galley left the harbour bound for home. Seeing how low they sat in the water, he wondered how many would actually make it.

From where he sat at the end of the breakwater he could hear the coarse naval commands and the babble of the crews' responses. He thought he detected a lightness, a relief in men's voices. A dangerous sea journey ahead for sure, but better than the certain death that they left behind.

He noted too that although galleys were entering the port there were many more leaving. He watched the wake of the last galley, straight as an arrow pointing westwards, and he realised that after all these years his future lay in that direction too. Finishing the last of his figs and tossing the empty wine skin into the clear blue waters he rose, turned, and strode down the breakwater towards the Venetian and Pisan quarters on the harbour front.

The harbour was crammed with galleys of all shapes and sizes. Some had sails furled neatly and bobbed tidily at anchor, whilst others had them thrown over their mizzen masts, their rigging a tangle of ropes. Men toiled endlessly, loading boxes and crates and rolls of cloth and silk; the merchants were in a feverish haste to

3

leave port. In the market adjoining the port the prevailing mood of uncertainty was less apparent as merchants and customers haggled loudly. The noise and bustle were strangely comforting in their normality. At one end of the port, beneath the Templar court, two galleys were moored. Their size and fitments marked them above the other ships bobbing in the crowded harbour. The outer vessel was clearly stood down, a solitary soldier pacing the forward deck beneath its expertly folded Mizzen sail. Her name in gold leaf glittered off the deeper blue of the harbour waters: *La Comptess*. This was The Knight Hospitaller's flagship. Next to her as Henri drew level was a similar vessel bearing the name *Bethania*, and it was to this ship his eyes were drawn.

A well-dressed lady was quarrelling with the tall knight on the quayside. Henri's lips compressed in disdain: Roger de Flor, a Templar knight, one he knew and disliked, and who, at the moment seemed to have only one God…the gold bezant, which was of course nothing unusual for a Templar.

'In God's name you cannot demand that,' she cried, her face suffused with anger.

Roger de Flor leant nonchalantly against a stay on the main mast. 'My lady, today it is 100 bezants, tomorrow it may be 200, or perhaps God willing, I will be gone, who knows?' His face smiled but his eyes flickered with greed.

Henri hardened his jaw and walked by, his urgent business unfortunately preventing him from interfering on this occasion. He left the couple still arguing as he made his way through the noisy throng. The crowd respectfully gave way before him catching sight of his red war mantle emblazoned with the white cross patee of the Knights Hospitaller. In the bustling streets with their street hawkers, children, off-duty soldiers, prostitutes and traders it was easy to forget that the city was under siege. People laughed, cried, nodded and haggled. Venetian prostitutes were pushed squealing into doorways by sweaty men; urchins and pickpockets ran up and down, bumping and jostling victims. Through it all Henri strode. He reflected that if you looked hard, really hard, you could see the shadow of fear in people's eyes. The city was living on the edge of the abyss, facing a ruthless and invincible enemy. He headed towards the outer curtain walls about two hundred yards from the Accursed Tower. There at St Anthony's Gate, he was to join in an attack that night on the Saracen army camped outside the City.

Unlike the mismanaged attempt of the Templars some two weeks previously, this raid would succeed, of that he was certain. That foray from the Gate of St Lazarus had been nothing short of disastrous.

The initial reason for the attack had been clear. One of Sultan Khalil's catapults, in fact his largest one, the *"Victorious"* had been positioned in front of the North wall defended by the Templars. Commencing on April 6th, the siege engine had been hurling huge rocks at the outer wall whilst its defenders cursed and swore impotently. An English knight, Otto de Grandison, had suggested a night-time sortie to set fire to this giant engine.

As dusk fell on the night of April 15th the streets around St Lazarus' Gate echoed to the clatter of hooves, the jangle of armour and the snorting of three hundred heavy warhorses. The sun, sinking westward into the darkening sea, slowly drew the light out of the day, so that at last all the waiting Muslim army could see beneath the city walls was an impenetrable blackness.

Under cover of this darkness the giant gate was unbarred and with its hinges previously greased with mutton fat, swung silently open. Three hundred horses streamed out from beneath the walls straight toward the unsuspecting Muslim army. In the last rays of the dying sun the giant siege engine could be seen surrounded by the tents and encampment of the Saracen. During the minutes it took to cover the ground between the walls and the enemy camp the light faded completely. Only the sound of thundering hooves could be heard. The lead horses crashed into the Muslim camp to the screams and yells of its utterly unprepared inhabitants. Unused to being attacked from the city, they had just settled down to an evening of feasting and relaxation when the mighty warhorses began to gallop into their camp. But in the planning of the attack something had been overlooked; the guy ropes of the closely packed tents, and the danger these would pose for the galloping horses. The first few stumbled over ropes, dragging the tents with them. Those behind, now blinded by the flapping billowing canvas, crashed into them. Onto the writhing, confused mass fell hundreds of outraged Muslim soldiers. The heavily armoured knights could not raise themselves from the tangle of ropes and horses and were slaughtered as they lay helpless.

Having thus lost the advantage of speed and weight the tiny force was virtually wiped out, costing the City a loss of armour and knights it could ill afford. The next morning, those who had managed to struggle back to safety had their wounds dressed and tended to.

The Muslim leader of the sector, al-Malik al Muzaffar, Lord of Hama, had the heads of the fallen Templars attached to their horses and sent back to the City, where the beasts were paraded up and down in front of the city walls, their gruesome cargo enraging the onlookers on the walls.

CHAPTER TWO

Nearing St Anthony's Gate, Henri resolutely pushed all thoughts of the massacre from his mind. He glanced around him; the narrow streets around the Gate were crowded and jostling with mounted Knights. He picked out the banners of the Knights of Lazarus, The Knights of the Realm of Sion, and his own troop of Knights Hospitaller, their crimson war mantles and white crosses contrasting with the blue mantles and black crosses of the small group of Teutonic Knights, with their Grandmaster Conrad von Feuchtwangen amongst them

He was pleased to see a number of the surviving Templars in their billowing white cloaks and crimson crosses talking in good spirits to a Knight of St Anthony in his black robe with blue Tau cross who was holding one of their distinctive double headed axes in his hand. Catching his eye, Henri raised a clenched fist in salute, a gesture returned by this swarthy knight. Seigneur Gilbert de Gothia Lord of Bezu had been with Henri since the fall of Marqab in 1285 and their adventures were talked of with awe over the length and breadth of the Holy Land.

Now the pair found themselves once more on the eve of battle facing the same old enemy. Henri's groom was waiting with his horse at the Gate. Nodding to him, Henri mounted the steps to the battlements. The streets' hubbub quietened beneath him as he arrived on the broad battlements above St Anthony's Gate. This part of the wall formed the apex of an inverted V. To his right stretched the battlements all the way to the Accursed Tower still being steadily battered by the Muslim catapults. To his left his own segment, the Hospitallers' Ward, looked peaceful and calm.   Henri St Gilles de Montfort, Titular Prince of Armenia Cyprus and

Jerusalem, Lord of Tyre, Toron, Tripoli and Antioch, and Lord of the French Estates of Montfort-l'Amaury and Castres, Knight Commander of The Hospitaller Order of St John of Jerusalem, was known to his friends and enemies alike as Henri the 'Lion', because apart from being a ferocious and brave warrior, his quartered arms bore the silver lion of the Montforts, the golden lion of Aquitaine and the red lions of Armenia and Cyprus. Henri leant on the battlements and surveyed the area to the east of the City of Acre. Tall and broad-shouldered, with a face burnt by the desert sun, he could have passed as an Arab. Only his square jawed features and piercing grey eyes betrayed his Norman French ancestry. He rested his bronzed forearms on the smooth sandstone and squinted across the plain. As far as the eye could see, in the light of the setting sun, human activity raised a low mist of dust over the plains. It had been suggested, and he had no reason to doubt it, that there were 160,000 Muslims camped around the last stronghold of Christendom in the Holy Land. Tents in bright, gaudy colours filled the horizon; the smoke of ten thousand campfires rose to the azure sky; groups of horsemen, light and fast, wheeled and turned in the dust in the distance. Occasionally he heard the deep bass *twang* of the catapults followed by a vibrating crash as the great rocks hit the wall.

His eyes sought the centre of this heaving, living horde. There was the tent of Sultan Khalil, its huge awning facing west so that all Muslims knew which way their Sultan was travelling. He could just make out tiny figures sitting on rich carpets in the tent's interior. Light sparkled off the silver goblets and plates as they ate. In the foreground of this mighty Infidel horde, just out of bow range of the archers, children of the Muslim army played mock battles as they re-enacted the tales of valour being told around the campfires behind them.

A group of children had completed a mock attack on another group and now had one of their number tied up and kneeling in the dust. The child wore a captured Templar mantle of white with the blood red cross plainly visible. Another child swung a glittering scimitar around his head and, as Henri's hands gripped the stone battlement, removed the captured knight's head. Shouting with glee, his high voice clearly audible in the still evening air behind him, he picked up the head and tossed it in the direction of the walls.

Henri's hands relaxed as the coconut, its rough surface crudely painted with human features bounced beneath him. The squeals of the children mocked him as they ran back to the brightly coloured tents. Watching their long legs flying over the rocks and scrub of the plain, his thoughts wandered, drifted and finally ended up where they always did; the Church at Tyre twenty-one years ago. A lifetime, it seemed, but the beginning of the losing of his whole family to the hated Saracen one by one.

✠ ✠ ✠

Twenty-one years ago, on August 17th, 1270, his beloved father, Philippe, Lord of Tyre and his two of his sons, Jean and Henri, had gone to the Church of the Holy Sepulchre in Tyre to worship. They always used their private Chapel off the nave of the main Church. Members of Philippe's bodyguard had stayed outside in the early morning sun playing quoits in the dusty square.

The three of them had entered the cool darkness of the Church and knelt in silent prayer. Henri, at twelve years of age, knew his father's capacity for prayer and the likely loss of feeling to his own knees. Not for Philippe the *effete* modern custom of kneeling on padded cushions in front of the altar. It was the stone floor for up to an hour.

Once Henri was sure his father's eyes were closed in supplication, he slowly rose from his knees and moved behind one of the large stone pillars supporting the timber roof. He still prayed, but from a more comfortable position—he was sure the Lord would understand. He closed his eyes and clasped his hands together. The silence of the Church grew as the minutes passed. Suddenly a door creaked. The rasp of metal cut through Henri's mood of quiet contemplation. Reflecting that he could still pray with one eye closed, he opened the other. Sunlight slanted into the church through the now open door. Soft, swift footsteps approached. Who was risking his Father's wrath by disturbing his prayers? Leaning forward to peer round the pillar he saw the tall form of Batu Al-Khalid, a Muslim who had converted to Christianity under the tutelage of his father's priest.

Batu had arrived in Tyre some four weeks' previously from the mountains, professing a desire to be converted. He had been accepted readily into the community of Tyre as an example of what the Christian faith could achieve over the Infidel. Now, Henri thought, he had obviously come to worship with his father, which was a mistake, as Philippe liked to pray in private. As Henri watched, Batu slowly and silently approached Philippe and Jean at the altar.

Nearing the kneeling figures, Batu's right hand disappeared into his robe. Steel flashed in the sunlight. Henri watched, unable to move, as the blade descended. His father rose, half turned, clutching at his throat. A glistening redness spread through his fingers. Batu struck again, the blade entering Philippe's chest. He fell heavily, his blood already spreading across the stone floor.

Jean, eyes wide in terror, screamed shrilly. At his cry the church door was flung wider and Philippe's bodyguard rushed in.

They found their master choking and agonising in a pool of blood. The assassin whirled to face the guards. Jean wavered uncertainly in between the dripping blade and the fast-approaching guard. Batu lunged at Jean but the boy was too quick and he hurled himself away from the flashing blade. Its tip caught his shoulder and a fine spray of bright red blood glittered for a moment.

Two of the guards had pinned the struggling assassin to the floor and another knelt over Philippe. His father's motionless body and the expression on the guards' faces told Henri everything. He had risen and backed away from the dreadful scene. One of the guard's rose from his knees and thrust his sword into the still wildly struggling assassin, who jerked spasmodically once and then lay still.

Suddenly a powerful arm had encircled Henri's body. A sweaty hand silenced his scream of terror. He choked on a smell of spices and herbs as he was dragged, kicking frantically, to the rear of the church. Then his head exploded in a burst of stars and bright lights and he sank into darkness.

CHAPTER THREE

The harsh jolting of the crude wooden cart brought him slowly back to consciousness. He was lying face down in a foul smelling mixture of straw and animal excrement. He tried to struggle up but found that he was bound hand and foot, but by the position of the setting sun he knew he was moving north.

The voices of his captors came to him over the rumbling of the wooden cart. They were the voices of men who had tasted success and who looked forward to returning home.

'Better to sell him in Sidon,' said one. 'A few bezants now would be better than waiting until Damascus.'

'No, Yousef, trust me. The boy will make a fine Mamaluke at Emir Baibars' camp, and the Emir will reward us, mark my words.'

Henri lay petrified. Mothers accompanying the Crusaders, in order to terrify infants into good behaviour had used the threat of "Baibars". Everyone knew the ferocious reputation of the former slave. Henri felt an overpowering sense of loneliness and grief steal over him. He began to weep uncontrollably.

His father, grandfather Guy, and his great uncle the infamous Simon de Montfort, had all felt the kiss of Saracen steel. When Henri was seven years of age, Baibars had personally executed 200 Templar Knights in front of the walls of Castel Safed, and followed that up two years later by the execution of over 1,000 soldiers outside Acre. Henri panicked briefly in his stinking, swaying prison, but suddenly he seemed to see the stern face of his father, and in spite of his despair he took deep calming breaths. Baibars would not be interested personally in the fate of a captured child, and of the two options the chance to be trained as a soldier, albeit for the opposing side, gave him the best hope of survival. It was a tradition that the Egyptians had started after they realised that the Turkish bowmen and horsemen, whilst brilliant in the field, packed up and went home when the money or job ran out. The meagre subsistence of the nomadic tribes was often strained by the birth of too many children, so that the young males between ten and twelve years were sometimes bought by the army to be trained in the use of the sword, horse, bow and battleaxe. Often little persuasion was needed, as the choice to be trained in one of the finest armies in the East was one which most young boys, given the alternative of herding goats for a lifetime, leapt at.

Young Henri, in his terror and anguish, instinctively knew that to survive he would have to appear as extremely promising fighting material from the moment his bonds were released.

The cart entered a body of water and was immediately flooded. For a moment Henri panicked. Then recovering his wits he gulped gratefully at the cool, fresh water, which, at the same time, was thankfully sluicing away most of the foul smelling detritus he was lying on. Refreshed, and now with the knowledge that they had crossed the River Litani to the north of Tyre, he relaxed, falling into a sleep of pure exhaustion.

Henri was released from his bonds as soon as the group reached the mountains above Damascus. He was then tied to the saddle of one of the Hashashin horses, for it was they who had kidnapped him after the bloody murder of his father. They had had no way of knowing that the small boy cowering behind the pillar was Philippe of Tyre's son. In their euphoria at the successful assassination of one of Christendom's most feared and ruthless Crusaders, they had grabbed the solitary child with nothing more in mind than selling him later to the highest bidder as a slave. Henri, remembering his thoughts on the subject, had fought savagely with his captors once his bonds were removed. He was restrained none too gently amidst much laughter and ribald comment, and by the time the group arrived at their mountain hideout all talk of selling him in the slave market had come to an end.

His neck halter remained, and he was issued with a flowing white jelabba like any young Arab boy. The group relaxed, comfortable in their mountain lair, and Henri was left to himself. He wandered aimlessly around the groups of huddled fighters as they talked and indulged in boisterous horseplay. They ignored him totally. When they cooked, someone would throw him scraps as they would to a dog. He felt utterly alone and dejected. After three days he was huddled in his cloak as near to the fire as he could get, when Yousef al Malik approached and sat beside him. After a long silence during which Yousef observed his young charge, he spoke.

'Tomorrow we start. Tomorrow we begin to make you a warrior.'

He nodded briskly and went striding away. The next morning the group began to school Henri in the art of battle.

An experienced and gifted horseman already, he took to the small light Arab horses as if he had been riding them all his life. Yousef-al-Malik, the leader of the small band who had urged caution about Henri's disposal on the first day of his capture, was especially keen to watch his young charge. One day Henri's halter was removed and he was given a small battleaxe mounted on flexible bamboo, which the Hashashin had adapted from those used by the Mongol army. Galloping down a small ravine at full speed, Henri had to remove a melon from the top of a pole stuck in the earth. At his first attempt he cleanly cut the melon in half. The watching band of Hashashin erupted into spontaneous applause. Henri made a mock bow to Yousef, but his eyes glittered with hatred. 'One day' he thought, 'the melon will be your head, Yousef al Malik'.

As a sect of the Shiites, the Hashashin had achieved an importance far above their actual military capability. Known as 'seveners' in Islam they believed that the missing seventh Imam, Ismail, would return as the 'Mahdi' or chosen one, being a blood descendant of the Prophet. Their sect had already slaughtered the fourth Imam, Uthman, hundreds of years earlier thus creating the Shiite movement, arguing that only descendants of the Prophet and not 'companions' should lead Islam. They claimed the right to slaughter anybody who stood in the way of their search for the Mahdi.

Henri had been seamlessly absorbed into this little mountain group led by the bearded Yousef al-Malik. He gradually realised that his birth in Tyre and life amongst the Arabs of the Christian Court had played a large part in saving his life. Dirty and evil-smelling as he was, there was little to distinguish him from a native-born Arab. He was, like most foreign aristocrats in the Holy Land, a fluent Arabic speaker, and understood fully the daily demands of the Muslim faith. Taking care to seek the East in order to pray five times a day, and eating only with his right hand, he was quickly absorbed into the band. When it was discovered he could shoot an arrow with considerable accuracy, so much that he could bring down a wild goat at over two hundred paces, he began to earn the grudging respect of the band of Hashishin.

The year passed quickly, and Yousef al Malik watched his charge mature into a tall strapping young man. One morning, in late spring, the group rose from their beds in the honeycomb of caves above the tumbling stream, and rather than the usual communal breakfast around the re-kindled camp fire, packed hard wheat cakes, figs and dates into their saddle rolls. In the distance, looking like a rolling bank of winter fog, a dust cloud approached. Normally for the group this would have signalled an instant dispersal. Not so today. The cloud became thousands upon thousands of men; walking, riding, carrying weapons and hauling huge siege engines. At its head, a group of a dozen horsemen, mounted on beautiful Arab stallions, rode up to greet Al-Malik. Whooping and yelling '*Allu, Allah al Akbar,*' [God is Great] they dismounted and embraced like long lost friends.

Yousef sought out the tallest and most brilliantly robed horseman, and after a few moments of boisterous laughter he turned to Henri and beckoned him. Henri stood patiently at Yousef's side, looking expectantly at the tall, arrogant leader before him. Piercing blue eyes, unusual in an Arab, regarded him from beneath black dense eyebrows. Henri felt a shiver run through him in spite of the morning sun.

'We acquired this little Mamaluke during our mission in Tyre,' Yousef said, 'I know of no finer bowman and horseman in my entire

15

troop. When he has sampled the delights of the seventy houris in heaven he will be a fearless soldier for the cause of Allah.'

The tall Emir nodded, grunting. He extended his hand to Henri.

'May I present Al-adin your eminence,' continued Yousef, using the name of the legendary Saladin's brother, which he had bestowed on Henri as a special honour. 'Al-adin, this is Sultan Rukn al-Din Baibars'.

Henri's hand had already been firmly grasped by Baibars. But at the sound of his name he recoiled. His eyes flashed hatred. Here was the very devil incarnate who had terrified Henri during his childhood; the man who had sent his assassins to murder Henri's father; the sole cause of the loss of his family's lands and their flight to the borders of the Mediterranean at Tyre.

He raised his eyes. They were without expression. He studied the man's face. He would remember it. In the confusion and general euphoria no one noticed him trembling as he fought to control his rage.

Henri's group joined the mighty caravan as it continued its journey north. Henri mingled with the soldiers at the head of the column. The mighty siege catapults of Baibars' army had been broken down into their separate parts, and it took over a thousand men to transport them. Progress was a painful five miles a day. The caravan's destination was the fabled Knights Hospitaller fortress of Krak de Chevaliers, a fortress enshrined in Muslim lore as the one that even the mighty Saladin had failed to conquer. But when after several weeks the huge cliff top fortress came into view the caravan merely wound its way along the valley floor. From the beleaguered but still defiant garrison came the loud, derisory blast of trumpets and clashing of symbols, followed by raucous laughter and catcalls as sewage and other waste was hurled down the cliffs at them.

Later, huddled round the campfire, Henri questioned Yousef as to the reason for passing the Fortress. Yousef smiled and nodded, pleased that his young charge had questioned the tactics.

'First Safita, then we come back for the Krak de Chevaliers. Sultan Baibars does not want to fight with another garrison at his back.'

At that time in late summer of 1271, Babairs' arrival at the smaller, light-coloured stone castle at Safita, sometimes known as Castel Blanc, had caught the defenders unaware. The garrison, under Templar Grand Master Thomas Berard, was seriously undermanned. In spite of its eleven-foot thick outer walls, the position was hopeless, given the overwhelming forces surrounding the fortress. Essentially Baibars required that the Fortress of Safita be neutralised so that he could concentrate on Krak de Chavaliers. He had opened negotiations with Thomas Berard and agreed that he and his Templars could leave, making their way back to Tortosa on foot. He surmised that news of his clemency would do him no harm in future negotiations. With Safita neatly out of the way, the column had returned to the business at Krak de Chavalier.

Henri darted around the engineers as they erected the giant catapults, and watched the quarrymen as they cut and hewed large pieces of rock with which to batter the walls. Brought up in fortresses and fortifications, he had a low opinion of the catapults in their ability to destroy walls many feet thick. These catapults were fashioned from timbers over a man's forearm thick. They took nearly a thousand men to transport them, and it took a week to erect them, three days merely to fill the trebuchet's large counterweight that gave the engine its power. Using a windlass manned by thirty brawny Egyptians, the giant arm was winched down and a large boulder of easily two men's weight placed in the basket. At a signal the windlass was released, and the counterweight plummeted to earth. The catapult's main shaft of over a man's torso in thickness could be seen to bend as the power of the counterweight was transferred to the end of the bucket. It needed as little effort as the flicking of a marble to make the huge boulder fly skywards. It crashed into the gatehouse of the mighty fortress so hard Henri felt it through his feet. Great lumps of shattered masonry began falling from the crenulations above the gate.

After a few days of incessant pounding the towers above the gatehouse were reduced to rubble. As the defenders retreated to avoid the falling masonry, the more agile of the Muslim archers climbed the walls either side of the huge gate. Fighting off frantic attempts to repel them, they managed to open the gate, and the leading groups of Muslim soldiers poured into the castle. Those who had not sought the sanctuary of the inner keep were doomed. Servants and native-born soldiers were shackled, and later sold into slavery. However, a group of thirty of so Hospitallers, some wounded, were taken prisoner. Henri stayed close to Yousef as he watched the group of proud knights being stripped naked and forced to kneel in the baking sun. Baibars had selected a patch of ground within the inner walls, but in full view of the remainder of the garrison clustered on the walls of the inner keep above him. The Sultan had his men erect his travelling tent, a gaudily striped affair, so that it's opening faced the inner keep of the watching Hospitallers. Parading up and down in front of the naked kneeling knights he offered them their lives if they renounced their god in favour of the one true Prophet by the time he had finished his afternoon refreshment. As he sat on his Persian carpet in the shade of his tent, he slowly sipped a goblet of effervescent sherbet. Draining the glass, he rose and took up a small knife and a pair of tongs used to place lumps of charcoal in the night braziers. Two huge gleaming Nubians dragged the first knight in front of the group, and forced him to kneel whilst holding his arms outstretched. Baibars approached the man and swiftly ran the knife down from his shoulders to his navel in two parallel strokes. The man screamed as blood spurted. Making a further sideways slashing movement Baibars now had a thin strip of skin cut on three sides from the victim's chest to his navel. Without pause he took the tongs and gripping the top of the flap of flesh he pulled the entire strip from the man. Without heeding the victim's screams he again slashed with the knife. The man was being skinned alive as the two impassive Nubians held him. Pausing when he had a pile of skin at the victim's knees he cut off a piece and forced it into the screaming knight's mouth. The horrific sounds died away slowly and the Nubians let their charge go. Twitching and moaning the knight bled and choked to death.

Every other Hospitaller was then beheaded in full view of the garrison.

For ten days they camped inside the inner walls. Then Baibars agreed that the garrison could leave without their weapons or food, and return to Tripoli on foot. This formed part of the legend of Baibars. Sometimes ferocious cruelty, other times he displayed something almost bordering on compassion. The message was clear to the inhabitants of the next city on Baibars' route.

There was good reason for Baibars' apparent softening of heart in not massacring the rest of the garrison. A new crusade led by the youthful but brilliant tactician, Prince Edward Plantagenet, accompanied by a certain Todaldo Viscont, had arrived in The Holy Land. In years to come these men would become Edward I of England and Pope Gregory X. Baibars had naturally little to fear from another few thousand crusaders, but the Mongols in the East under their supreme leader Kublai Khan were stirring again. Baibars had already received threatening communication from Kublai's son, the Ilkhan Abaga, demanding that the Egyptians bow to the Mongol Khan. Thomas Berard, the Templar Grand Master and recipient of Baibars 'mercy' at Safita, had good reason to believe a treaty with Baibars was possible. All this intelligence came to Henri via his fireside lessons from his mentor Yousef. One night Yousef had joined Henri at the dying remains of the campfire. The group had eaten well, and drunk large quantities of Kumis, so that the fire was surrounded by sleeping men.

The two were now left on their own. Yousef leant towards Henri conspiratorially. Since Henri's acceptance by the group he was treated almost as an equal.

'Very soon I shall have my seventy virgins in Heaven my friend.'

Yousef's expression was unreadable. Henri looked at him questioningly.

'I have been given a mission by Baibars himself,' the other man went on. 'I am to go to the court of Prince Edward of England and ingratiate myself into his company, then...'

Yousef paused and glanced quickly over his shoulder before removing a small bundle from his cloak. It contained a wickedly curved dagger. He wrapped it up quickly and returned it to the folds of his garment.

'And you are to accompany me! Though you need not sample the virgins just yet,' he added wryly.

He was to take his young Mamaluke Al-adin as witness, and as part of his manhood initiation rite. Yousef's eyes gleamed in the darkness as the promise of eternity with seventy virgins beckoned. The boys and young men of the camp had, of course, discussed these matters loudly and at length with the young Henri.

At certain times the normal day-to-day routines of the group were suspended, and they sat around all day smoking hashish or eating it baked into sweet cakes. One or two of the group, usually the boys aged eighteen or nineteen, and sprouting wispy hairs of manhood, were fed more than the rest. When virtually unconscious they were taken further up the valley to a small walled area around a splashing mountain stream. In their advanced hallucinatory state they found themselves alone and naked in a lush walled garden, with six or more beautiful young, sexually accomplished women called houris. All day these women would tend to their every whim and need, including some they had never heard of before. When the effect of the hashish eventually wore off the girls would have disappeared, and the young men's incredulous tales to their compatriots would be gravely interpreted as a vision of heaven, available to all young Muslims for all eternity if they sacrificed themselves in the name of God. Yousef had now been given his own personal Jihad by Sultan Baibars himself and was ready to die.

CHAPTER FOUR

The peace treaty with Prince Edward was not thirty days old when Yousef and Al-adin were sent to his court at Tortosa. As a senior emir from the Sultan himself, Yousef was received warmly into the English court, accompanied by Henri in the guise of his page. Yousef professed to be negotiating the finer details of the ten-year treaty with Baibars. At the same time he was ingratiating himself, and portraying himself as secretly admiring the Christian faith. After a few weeks, Yousef and Henri's attendance at the daily Mass attracted scant attention, and Edward spent many hours with Yousef discussing the finer points of Christianity versus Islam. Eventually he dropped his guard sufficiently to allow himself to be in Yousef's company outside his quarters, with only the minimum number of bodyguards

One morning Henri awoke to find Yousef on his prayer mat, facing east and holding the long thin dagger, whose blade he could now see was discoloured. With sudden realisation he knew it was poisoned. He watched in fascination as Yousef prepared himself for the journey into the afterlife that the assassination of Prince Edward would bring for him.

For several days Yousef had gone alone to the royal quarters in order to distance himself from Henri. The plan was for Henri to witness the murder of Edward, then escape and report back to Baibars himself. Accordingly he dressed himself in a scruffy jellaba so that he was indistinguishable from any other young man around the castle. He positioned himself at the far end of the courtyard, and busied himself around the water trough. Letting the horses drink, he watched as Yousef swiftly entered the royal apartments.

A scream of pain and a bellow of anger brought the guards pounding across the courtyard. Henri went racing towards the Royal quarters followed by the Prince's young wife. A small but growing group of courtiers, bodyguards and personal retainers had begun to gather around an inert form on the marble floor. Edward was laying there, his robes ripped from him.

The Princess pushed her way through the crowd and knelt at her husband's side, ordering everybody away as she did so.

'Water! Quickly!' she cried. She held up the knife. It was the one Henri had seen earlier in Yousef's hand. Only the tip was stained with blood, showing that the penetration into Edwards's body had been minimal. To Henri's astonishment she bent her head and covered the bloody gash beneath Edward's ribs with her lips. Her body heaved, and she spat a stream of blood and spittle onto the pale marble floor.

The crowd had parted in obedience to the Princess's command, and Edward twisted his head to look at the soldiers holding Yousef, whose face had taken on a dreamlike calmness. He raised his arm and pointed.

'Guilty!' He managed to croak. 'Execute the heathen bastard now!' Then he slumped backwards, unconscious.

Yousef was dragged roughly into the courtyard. His eyes caught Henri's and he smiled in complete happiness. He was still smiling as he was forced to his knees; smiling still as the swift sword removed his head and sent it rolling in the dust.

Henri shrank into the gathering crowd and headed towards the castle gates. He walked in the heat without feeling, his mind numb. It was only after several miles that his thoughts calmed. Even though Yousef and his group had kidnapped him during the most appalling event in his life, whether Henri wanted to admit it or not, Yousef had been relatively kind to him and kept him safe. Also he had taught him skills that would help him considerably in his future life. Yet the shock of the brutal removal of Yousef's head faded somewhat as he remembered his own Father's death. With renewed strength he took the road to the mountains again.

Some days later Henri stood shaking in front of the tall figure of Sultan Baibars. Baibars' emirs regarded with some amusement the ragged dirty sixteen year old, dusty from the long road from Tortosa.

'Sit, sit my child,' Baibars said slowly, his eyes glittering. 'Did you see the Prince breathe his last?'

'No, no,' Henri, whispered. 'I did not; lord, but I saw how his lady held up the bloodstained dagger in her hand.

'But Yousef is in paradise?'

'Oh, yes, Lord, executed on the spot.'

Baibars turned briefly to a hawkish looking emir next to him.

'Go! Confirm Edward's death. An assassin should leave no room for doubt'.

Turning again to Henri, he smiled benignly. 'Go now with our thanks. Rest, refresh yourself. You have done well.' Relieved, Henri stumbled from the tent.

If there was doubt in Sultan Baibars' mind about the outcome of the assassination, there was none in the camp of the Hashashin. They danced and whirled the night away to the relentless thump of the kettledrums as the campfire burned brightly, hurling effervescent sparks towards the inky heavens now alight with a thousand stars. Henri sat on the edge of the group, neither with them nor apart from them. He had survived the last few years, and he was grateful to the Hashashin for that. It had been better than a life sold into slavery. But his thoughts had increasingly of late turned to the moment of his capture, and to memories of his father, never perhaps a warm figure, but a tower of stability and strength, who had run his fiefdom in Tyre with a firm but fair hand, and who had been slain at a moment of prayer by a murderous Infidel. And like an echo of that evil event, Prince Edward, stabbed by a man in his confidence for whom, just for a moment, he had let his guard down.

Henri spat in the dust and clenched his fists. His toes were gritty with sand and his lice-infested jelabba itched unbearably. He suddenly had a vision of his quarters in the keep at Tyre; fresh water from the well, meals on tables in front of roaring fires, and the basic simplicity of his privileged life. He lowered his head and his eyes glittered in the darkness. He clenched and unclenched his fists. Suddenly the tears came.

In the morning he joined his group as they prepared to return to their mountain lair. They did not exist as a standing army, but if Sultan Baibars needed their services again, he knew where to find them. Henri set off with the group, galloping with them towards the distant purple mountains. He knew now what he had to do. One slip and he was dead, but if it took a lifetime, he had to return to his family and take his rightful place. Only from there could he be certain of avenging his father's death. He whooped and cried with his fellow Hashashin as the dust rose around their horses flying hooves, but his heart beat steadily and coolly as they thundered into the band's mountain lair.

According to custom, the responsibility of the training and equipping of Henri passed to Yousef's brother Ayub al Malik. Whilst an accomplished soldier Ayub was not as communicative as his late brother so that once each day's training and skirmishing had come to an end, Henri found himself at a loose end around the camp.

Whilst the group of fifty or sixty Hashashin formed an independent unit, they kept themselves abreast of intelligence via a network of spies, not only in Baibars' camp, but in the Christian strongholds and the Mongol army, ever present and threatening to the east. In the summer or early autumn of 1276, Sultan Baibars sent word to the senior Hashashin, of which Ayub was one, that he was to move on to the Cyptiot land of Anatolia to the north. The recent death of the Seljuk leader had left a four-year old on the Sultan's throne, controlled by a greedy Emir named Suleiman. Whilst he paid tribute to the Mongol Ilkhan Abaga, who prudently kept a garrison of horsemen in his country, he helped himself to the country's riches, and ignored the plight of the people. Sultan Baibars had perceived this opportunity and promptly invaded. Whilst the Hashashins were not part of the invasion, they were always kept fully informed in case their services should be required.

Baibars moved on Anatolia, seeing little threat from the small Mongol garrison. However, news of his success reached the ears of the Ilkhan Abaga, and in fury he mobilised the entire Mongol army. Sultan Baibars was a brilliant tactician, and a courageous leader, but even he feared the gathering Mongol hordes. Quickly he retired into Syria. In the heart of Damascus, in 1277, Baibars burned with rage. Not only had he had to give way to the Mongol army, but also a young Syrian prince, al-Qahir, was receiving more than his fair share of praise for the recent military actions. Baibars was acutely aware that the Prince was a descendent of the legendary Saladin, and finally he could contain his anger no longer. The young al-Qahir, now invested as the Prince of Kerak, was invited to a grand banquet. Henri's group was also invited, in case their particular skills should be required.

Over five hundred people sat down under the stars to feast and consume vast quantities of Kumis, the fermented mare's milk that was so highly regarded by the Mongols.

As the evening wore on, Sultan Baibars and the young prince staggered about among the royal entourage in a display of affection and respect. Henri had one of the large leather gourds, and was replenishing drinks as fast as he could. He approached Sultan Baibars, who by this time was used to his presence, and had been for a number of years.

Baibars had collapsed onto a large silk cushion, and the young prince had done the same. Both men's eyes were struggling to stay open. As Henri bent with the gourd, Baibars fumbled under his cloak. He held in his unsteady hand a small phial containing a milky liquid. Henri watched, mesmerised, as Baibars' fingers crushed the top of the phial. His left hand pointing unsteadily, he drew the Prince's attention to a group of beautiful young houris dancing nearby. With the other hand Baibars quickly tipped the contents of the phial into al-Qahir's goblet. Reacting almost without thinking, Henri smoothly removed the goblet from the Prince's hand. The young man, his eyes still fixed on the houris, could see nothing else.

Henri now took the drunken Baibar's goblet, and with his back half turned, made as if he was refilling it. Substituting it for the poisoned chalice, he turned back offering it to Baibars. He waited until Baibars had swallowed a deep, full draft of the poison, then moved on past the recumbent Emirs and the snoring soldiers to the campfire. He sat in the glow of the fire behind the shelter of a group of sleeping men. Around him the camp quietened down for the night, the odd snoring or guttural retching of someone vomiting being the only sounds in the inky blackness. He dozed fitfully, his mind alive.

The first screams of terror and anguish woke everybody in the camp. In the ensuing confusion it was not immediately clear that they came, not from one throat, but from two. As the soldiers, still dazed with drink, milled about in anxious disorder, first the Sultan, and then the young prince, al Qahir, emerged, staggering and stumbling, from their tents, hands tearing at their bodies in fearful agony.

Their skins glistened with sweat and their eyes were swollen to twice their normal size. Against their pallor the whites of their eyes stood out as they howled and writhed in torment. Clutching at their stomachs they collapsed at last and lay still in the grit of the desert.

Henri watched with a strange feeling of detachment as Baibars' emirs tried, with one potion after another, to revive the all but lifeless forms. As dawn streaked the sky, first the young prince, and then Sultan Baibars, howled and breathed their last. Henri, clenching his fists, watched in triumph knowing that Christendom's most ruthless enemy in the Holy Land was now dead.

Henri slipped away into the darkness and made his way back to his own people, taking with him the skills of a trained assassin that he would now use against his mortal enemies.

CHAPTER FIVE

Had it really all happened so long ago?

Fourteen years had passed, during which time the Holy Land *should* have been won back from the Infidel. Henri ground his teeth, hands clenching on the stone battlements, as his eyes took in the Muslim hordes led by Khalil camped just three hundred yards from the walls of Acre.

It would take no less than a miracle for them to fail to push the Christians into the sea at Acre. This was last bastion of Christianity in the Holy Land, now just a breath away from extinction.

Henri's thoughts grew darker as the sun sank towards the sea. For years, under the continual onslaught of the Infidel, the Holy Land had fragmented, each part ruled separately by the various Chivalric orders, all in direct competition with each other. They stupidly preferred to war with each other rather than concentrate on keeping the Heathens from the Gate. How had Pope Urban II's rallying call from Clermont proved so fruitless?

Henri took a deep breath, straightening his shoulders. He looked forward to the coming combat. He had spent most of his life in one battle or another since he had escaped from the Hashashin after assassinating Sultan Baibar all those years ago. But tonight, although he was confident in his planning of the skirmish, he felt certain pessimism. He doubted that the raid would really affect the result of the coming battle for Acre. He watched the Saracens around their campfire as they squatted on the ground beating their large copper kettledrums. The rhythm began to increase as their excitement and euphoria grew. Their eyes would be glittering with hatred, and their teeth would be bared. Jubilant, they knew that only a few stones stood between them and the last Christians in the Holy Land. The end was not in doubt. It was merely a matter of time.

Henri's thoughts drifted back to when his mother, Princess Maria of Armenia, after her initial joy at her reunion with her youngest son, seemingly back from the dead, had encouraged Henri to join the Knights Hospitaller under Jean de Villiers. She had inherited her late husband's conviction that the Templars, with their posturing and quarrelling, had cost Christendom the Holy Land. In her own capacity as Princess of Antioch, she had met a previous Hospitaller Grand Master, the thoughtful and subtle Hugues de Revel, before his death in 1277. As a direct result of that meeting, Henri had found himself fighting at the side of a certain Gilbert de Gothia at the siege of Marqab 1285. It was not only to be the start of a lifelong friendship, but would also change Henri's life forever. Henri's mind drifted further as he remembered the occasion that had forged their friendship.

Sultan Khala'un's catapults had been battering the Gatehouse at Marqab all that morning, whilst his archers had kept up a deadly hail of arrows. Simultaneously, under this cover, his miners were excavating the rock beneath the castles foundations. The truth was that whilst the catapults had proved a small success, the height of the fortress of Marqab, mounted as it was on a rocky promontory, meant that they expended most of their force throwing the rocks upwards. With this in mind, Kala'un had ordered the use of thousands of miners, who had been cutting away at the cliff beneath the walls. When they had enlarged a sufficient area, they propped up the roof under the castle foundations with pitch and naptha soaked timbers. Eventually the creaks and groans told them that the weight of the foundations was now supported solely by these wooden props. The props were then set on fire. Far above the miners the garrison could smell the vapours of the naptha as it was being poured on the tunnel's props, and feel the vibrations of the miners beneath their feet.

To reconnoitre, Henri had braved the showers of arrows, and had just reached the battlements when a particularly large boulder crashed into the wall in front of him.

As Henri leapt forward over the falling masonry, a rumbling came from under his feet. Incredibly, an enemy foot soldier appeared suddenly before him. Henri, slowed by his bulky armour, was a fraction later than the other man in recovering the initiative. As the swarthy warrior's scimitar swept murderously upwards, somewhere from Henri's right came a bellow of warning, and the blade was deflected by a blow from a double-headed battleaxe.

The same weapon, continuing its deadly arc, disappeared into the face of Henri's assailant. Henri was pulled backwards over the fallen stones. Recovering swiftly and fighting to raise his sword arm against this unknown force, his struggles were cut short by a tremendous roar. The timely action of Gilbert de Gothia, had saved Henri from disappearing into the enormous hole where the gatehouse and ramp to the castle once stood. This same hole had prevented any further incursions into the castle, and as a result both sides retired to plan the next move. After three days, Sultan Kala'un called a truce and, to the knights' astonishment, gave terms that each knight could leave with his horse, armour and personal weapons, whilst the foot soldiers were to leave with nothing.

Henri had, of course, witnessed this kind of diplomacy under Baibars, and appreciated the game the Sultan played. When the hungry knights and soldiers found their way back to Tripoli, Sultan Kala'un would not be seen in too unfavourable a light, and this would make the defence of a large city difficult if there was seemingly little to fear from the Saracen hordes. As the disconsolate knights and foot soldiers streamed slowly out of Marqab, Kala'un's masons had begun dismantling the mighty fortress stone by stone. Henri, Gilbert de Gothia, and what was left of the garrison wound their way down the mountain track. The stones that the masons hurled down the cliffs bounced and reverberated along the valley. The pair rode side by side without speaking until the noise of the destruction faded in the distance.

'The road to Tripoli is long, Henri,' muttered Gilbert.

'And there is only the sea beyond that,' rejoined Henri.

The pair lapsed again into an uneasy silence. Henri felt waves of alternate rage and despair wash over him. He sat slumped in his saddle, caring little if a loose Saracen arrow should find its mark. He was twenty-nine years old. He bore his father's title of Lord of Tyre. He had inherited his mother's estates in Armenia, Antioch, and Tripoli and his elder brother Philippe's estates in France, of Montfort L'Amaury, Ferte-Alais and Castres, following his recent death in Tunisia. He was, in theory at least, a fantastically wealthy and highly placed young man. Again and again the Templars had retreated, conceded or been beaten back towards the sea. Those taken prisoner had either been killed on the spot or sold later as slaves. To be sure, Henri had tasted his share of victories but they had been battles won in a losing war. His mother had barely been restored to him when she was cruelly murdered in a Muslim raid. Before she died, she had been raped by a succession of drunken Cyptiot bowmen.

Three years later his elder brother, Jean of Toron, had died in a fight with Muslim traders in the Port of Tripoli, and finally, so had Humphrey, his closest brother, the year before the fall of Marqab, now the only family he had, lived far away in France and England.

The memory of Humphrey's death was still painful and fresh to Henri, and now he was the last of the de Montfort family left in this godforsaken land. But he had inherited one thing from his family — a steely determination to overcome his enemy. The one thread that had run through his life so far had been the desire for violent contact with the followers of the Prophet Mohammed. His father, his mother, his three brothers, gone now, murdered by the Infidel, and aided not a little in his eyes, by the incompetence, greed and internecine rivalry of the Knights Templar.

And then the blackness in his heart had been suddenly replaced by a burning passion; a heat so fierce it made him grip his sword, force himself upright in his saddle and swear silently that he would not rest until the forces of Mohammad were defeated and pushed back to the burning barren sands of Arabia. He had glanced across at Gilbert.

They had met only in the last weeks of the siege at Marqab but already each man felt a deep sense of brotherhood towards the other. There had been times in battle when death threatened, and each had found the other at his side. Gilbert had caught Henri's glance; he had seen the fury in his friend's eyes. Then Henri's anger faded as he threw off his black mood and the pair smiled briefly at each other, tight lipped.

'The first to Tripoli buys dinner', shouted Henri, digging his spurs to his charger's flank. Gilbert did likewise and the two galloped past the despondent column, heading towards the glittering ocean in the far distance. Roaring and whooping, the two exorcised their gloomy thoughts and exchanged them for the promise of good food in Tripoli…

✠✠✠

Henri now pushed these crowding thoughts and memories to the back of his mind, and turned to make his way back along the battlements. He saw a figure approaching, and paused, recognising the familiar gait.

'Gilbert, dearest friend how are you tonight?' he called.

Gilbert bowed mockingly. 'Ready to blunt my sword on the Saracen's head, my Prince.'

The two men embraced warmly. These last five years since Marqab had seen them grow and mature together. Gilbert de Gothia had in many ways become a surrogate brother to Henri, and the two were seldom apart. Gilbert, a Knight Commander of the Order of St Anthony, had parried and teased Henri's probing questions about his Order, giving little away. On the occasions that the two were parted, Henri had from time to time found his friend wandering around the oldest churches of Acre, and the chapel at the Gate of St Anthony where they now stood. As the pair stood down from various forays, especially in the last twelve months, Gilbert's journeys to the other churches in Acre had become more frequent. Henri had questioned his friend but to little avail, save that Gilbert's apparent quest appeared to have begun from the moment a messenger from his home in Villandraut, in France, had delivered a letter to him. All that Henri had discovered was that he lost his father in a jousting tournament when he was 4-years old and, had been adopted by his uncle Bishop Bertrand de Gothia who lived at Chateau Villandraut and that he had a sister, Eleanor, that he loved deeply, who was versed in the healing arts, and was newly arrived in Acre.

Gilbert leant on the battlements, blocking Henri's path. He nodded in the direction of Khalil's tent.

'See the chest with the carrying poles next to Khalil?'

It was a statement as much as a question. Henri stared at the Infidel encampment and grunted in acknowledgement, his brow puckering.

'That would be a greater prize than setting fire to a catapult,' he said. Gilbert spat in derision.

'That chest carries the world's first written Koran by Uthman, who was murdered whilst reading it in 656.'

Henri's frown deepened. Up until now he had assumed that Gilbert's off-duty knowledge was restricted to eating and wenching. Gilbert continued, his voice deepening, 'You may think, my Prince, that a unified army of Islam opposes us. Nothing could be further from the truth. The Koran in that tent, not more than a thousand yards away, was written by the third Caliph after Ali, called Uthman. As he sat writing in the book he was murdered by the followers of Ali, who claimed that the word of God should pass down the bloodline direct from Mohammad. That Holy Koran is still stained with Uthman's blood. After his murder it was rumoured the Koran was taken to Ethiopia, the original homeland of the Knights of St Anthony. Subsequently the Islamic empire expanded at an incredible rate. Within 76 years of Uthman's death in Mecca, the Infidel had conquered northern Africa and Spain and had begun to move into Aquitaine and Gaul.'

'Fortunately for our holdings in France,' Gilbert continued wryly, 'our ancestors under Charles Martel defeated Al Ghafiqi at the Battle of Poitiers in 732. That Koran was at the battle and narrowly avoided capture at the hands of Martel's troops. Some of the group of Muslims carrying the Koran whilst fleeing back to Andalusia disappeared in the Languedoc, and it was rumoured that part of their Holy Koran went missing during a skirmish in that area too.'

'Go on,' Henri said glancing curiously at his friend.

Gilbert continued, 'There are two forces opposing us, my Lord; the followers of Ali who was a direct descendent of the Prophet—I believe they call themselves the Shi'at Ali or Ahl al Boyt, and the followers of Uthman who call themselves Sunni.'

Gilbert fell silent. Henri was surprised to see by his friend's expression that there was a struggle going on within him. Gilbert began again, his voice lower, 'There are some who say the contents of Uthman's Koran, if it is complete, could divide the Infidel in a manner that would make our battle for the Holy Land seem a child's game. I don't know if this is true. But one thing is certain. Seize that Holy Koran and you will split the heathen forever.'

If Henri wondered where his friend had obtained this knowledge he did not say, but he thought if the foray tonight got anywhere near the Sultan Khalil, it would be worth a fight to win their Sacred Book.

The pair continued to chat companionably on the walls as the blood-red sun sank into the darkness of the sea. Then gathering themselves, they made their way down the narrow unguarded steps into the throng of men and horses waiting behind the Gate of St Anthony. Gilbert preceded Henri, his dark cloak and blue Tau cross merging so that he cut a dark and menacing figure. The throng of tense armed soldiers parted as the two made their way through the crowd; Henri and Gilbert had a reputation for enjoying a hard fight. Men respected them.

Henri sometimes felt Gilbert held back from describing the Anthonines, although nominally under Hospitaller command he knew that they also had some kind of Papal favour. He felt glad that Gilbert was fighting by his side. However, thinking of the imminent raid he suddenly felt an inexplicable sense of unease.

As usual he and Gilbert were in the vanguard of the knights, and he watched the gleaming, sweating torsos of the gatekeepers as they pulled back the oiled timbers holding the doors closed. The doors swung inwards silently, and a cool breeze fanned the waiting horsemen. Not four hundred yards away, the fires from the enemy camp glimmered in the darkness. Some three weeks previously, the raiding party of Templar Knights had been tripped up by the guy ropes of the Infidel tents as they crashed into them with predictably fatal results. Henri had given this problem some thought, and after much experimentation, he had lashed a small flexible bamboo-handled battleaxe, spoils of war from a Mongol soldier, to a section of broken lance. He discovered he could ride at a tent and, whirling the now extended axe round his shoulders, effectively cut any guy ropes before his horse tripped on them. The further honing of this technique had led Gilbert and Henri to create an arrow formation of horsemen, with the outer edge comprising more agile local horsemen wielding these axes. In the centre of the group rode the armoured knights.

Obeying muted commands, the battle group formed up in the deep shadow of the walls. Eschewing the usual bellowed battle cries the formation moved off on a steady canter, building to a full gallop as the last rays of the dying sun lit the scene. Henri crouched on his black stallion, the warm evening air streaming through the slit in his visor. This was his world, and he revelled in it.

With the creak and jangle of the galloping armoured Knights loud in his ears, he focussed on the darkened encampment ahead. Through his wind-seared eyes, he saw the angular shapes of the Muslim army's tents come into view. He urged his mount onwards, and the bunched arrow formation loosened a little. Now his blood was up and he raised his sword, anticipating the bloody havoc he would wreak with it. The tents were now only seventy yards away. He could make out the individual campfires, and soldiers passing to and fro before them. Suddenly his straining eyes detected something else. Small pinpricks of light were moving rapidly and erratically along the line of tents. With some difficulty he made out shadowy forms holding flaming torches.

The Infidel army had perfected the art of using naphtha oil obtained from underground deposits in Persia. They had often used it to great effect to fire the timbers supporting crusader castle walls that they had mined. Henri's mind, finally grasping the enemy's intention, was a fraction too late in warning him of the danger. As the soldiers touched their flaming torches to the ground, lines of bluish flames leapt towards the galloping horses. The flattened area before the enemy camp was lit up, showing criss-cross channels filled with the flaming substance. Where the lines intersected, small piles of brushwood burst into flames in front of the galloping formation. Henri tried to rein his mount in, but it was far too late. The horses on the edge of the formation turned in panic at the approaching conflagration. Screaming with terror, the lighter horses collided with the heavier Destriers of the Knights at the centre. Speed, weight and momentum ensured that the smaller horses were rammed and trampled by the armoured chargers. Henri tried vainly to rein in his horse as it collided violently with another. The impact splintered the other rider's leg. He screamed in agony, and was thrown to the ground, to be crushed to a bloody pulp by his own falling horse. In the confusion Henri now heard an altogether more sinister noise—the whirr and hiss of hundreds of arrows as the Cyptiot bowmen stepped out from behind their tents.

He knew in an instant what he must do. His armour and horse were only of any use on the move, and at speed. Slowed to a halt, surrounded by fallen, struggling men, there could be only one outcome. He wheeled to his left as Gilbert did likewise; as always the pair acted uncannily as one in the heat of battle, Henri had completed his left wheel, and was searching for a gap in the chaos towards which he and Gilbert could head. The last of the dying sun had illuminated the skyline of Acre, and Henri flattened himself along his charger's back and dug his spurs in. As he did so, a metallic twang reverberated around his head, and an arrow bounced off his steel helm. He grinned grimly in the darkness as his horse turned and flew back to the safety of Acre.

The second arrow made no noise. He felt a searing, red-hot agony low down on his right side. The pain took his breath away. His fingers loosened on the reins. He felt himself falling. Strangely, as he hit the ground the pain disappeared, and for a moment he felt that he was floating on his back as he looked up at the star-filled sky. His breath came back suddenly in great shuddering gasps. Dimly he heard horses being drawn to a halt and the rattle of armour as dark figures surrounded him. He felt hands lift him and he shouted in agony as the blackness descended.

CHAPTER SIX

He didn't know how long he'd been unconscious. He felt his brow being wiped gently with a blessedly cool cloth. He heard Gilbert say, 'The arrow must have broken when we put him on the horse, sister.'

'We must remove the arrow before putrefaction sets in,' a female voice said firmly. It continued conversationally; 'Did you capture the Koran of Uthman?'

Henri at this point opened his eyes and saw Gilbert shake his head at someone he couldn't see. Then a female figure came into view as she leaned over him. She rolled him onto his side and a blinding, searing pain shot through him. This woke him fully. The woman continued, 'See, the arrow has only penetrated his flesh, the barbs are just below the skin—we must cut around the head of the arrow using the Egyptian spoons, and draw the whole shaft through his skin.'

Henri's pain came again, stronger this time, and he felt himself floating away.

Gilbert looked at the fresh-faced nun. A smile lifted the corners of his lips. His younger sister had arrived by boat in the besieged city the week before. He and Eleanor had grown up together under the protection of their uncle and godfather, Bertrand de Gothia, back at the Castle of Villandraut in France. Ostensibly she had arrived at the beleaguered port of Acre to care for the wounded Knights. Gilbert however knew that the news of his discovery of the ancient manuscripts and bound volumes of the Treasury of St

Anthony would have caused his uncle Bertrand de Gothia to send his sister to take it back to France.

Her eyes, a deep intense blue, shone and sparkled at her sunburnt swarthy brother, tall and lean from years of fighting in the Outremer sun. 'If you want your friend to live, my brother, we need to cut him now and remove the arrow.' She looked hard at Gilbert.

'You have our book now, haven't you?'

He nodded mutely.

'We may need some of the knowledge it contains, if we are to stop this wound putrefying.'

Eleanor moved to the curtain over the doorway of the small chamber where they had laid Henri. Sweeping it to one side she motioned in one of Henri's troop, and bade him stand at the foot of the wooden table upon which Henri lay. Stooping, she picked up a small leather bag, taking out a long apron, which she tied around herself. Rolling Henri onto one side, she motioned Gilbert to hold his arms, whilst the soldier was pressed into holding his legs. 'Firmly, man, firmly!' she snapped, 'This Knight looks very strong.'

Eleanor bent over Henri, and with a sharp knife cut his woollen vest to the armpit, exposing his finely muscled torso. The arrow had entered Henri's body below his breastplate, but above the rear pommel of his large saddle, nicking his side as he twisted away from the flaming naphtha. A bloody haft of splintered wood protruded from his back. The line of the shaft could plainly be seen beneath his taut flesh. The larger protuberance of the arrowhead was visible below his ribcage in a small roll of body fat. Eleanor's fingers traced the arrow, feeling the beginnings of the heat of putrefaction. She pulled a small blade and a pair of long narrow bronze spoons from her bag.

The ancient Egyptians had pioneered the use of these spoons, primarily to extract the contents of the skull prior to mummification, and their use was fully explained in the manuscripts and volumes that Eleanor's brother had found. These were, amongst other things, a treasury of healing knowledge that had been gradually added to since the time of St Anthony, the patron of the Order to which she and her brother belonged.

The Order was currently under the control of Bertrand de Gothia, Bishop of Bordeaux, their uncle and Grand Prior of the Order. Although it had strong links to the Papacy, it had in fact, been founded in Ethiopia in 370 AD by the local king, Prester John, for the defence of Christianity, and was the oldest Order of Chivalry in Christendom. That part of the world had been under enormous influence from the ancient Egyptians, and the use of bronze spoons in surgery was well developed from the time of the Pharaoh's.

The volumes also recorded the early beginnings of Islam, and the turmoil created in Mecca and Medina following the murder of the Caliph Uthman in 656, when elements of the Infidel fled to Ethiopia with the first written Koran. It was Uthman's writings that were of great interest to the Order.

Eleanor's fingers sought beneath the skin for the sharp tip of the arrow. She made a small cut across the skin, digging deeply until she felt the blade strike something hard. Henri convulsed on the table. 'Hold him!' she snapped, as she worked the twin spoons deep into his flesh guiding their shapes around the barbed arrowhead. With one hand she held the two spoons as they cocooned their deadly cargo, and with the other she enlarged the slit her knife had made. Henri writhed and moaned. 'Hold him down!' she shouted, and pulled strongly upwards with the spoons. Henri's body twisted, and he bellowed in pain, but Eleanor triumphantly held aloft the bloody remains of the arrow shaft. Dropping the spoons into a small dish, she took a pitcher of clear water and poured it into the wound. It flowed from both wounds bloody and streaked with clots of dark venous blood. She continued to pour until the water ran clear. Taking a handful of Hypericum leaves mixed with potassium crystals she packed them in the wound and wrapped a long bandage around Henri's torso, stretching round his girth as she fed the bandage under him, her cheeks pressed to the damp curls on his slowly breathing chest. She rose and looked at Gilbert.

'Rest for ten days—he mustn't leave his bed.'

Without waiting for a reply she swept out of the room. Gilbert watched her depart before turning back to the sweat drenched form of his friend.

Eleanor came back each day to change Henri's dressing. She was alarmed to see after the second day a trickle of weak pus seeping from his wound. She administered more of the purple potassium crystals, and for good measure, smeared his wound with wild honey and garlic. All these cures she had found in The Treasury of St Anthony that her brother had recovered for The Order. Within ten days the wound had dried and a firm crusty covering had appeared.

If Henri wondered why Eleanor had come to Acre at such a dangerous time, he refrained from enquiring. The news reaching his hospital bed was disastrous, and he fretted and became impatient with his immobility. Eleanor would not countenance his rising from his bed, and he found this female authority over him frustrating. Outside the walls a seething mass of Infidel soldiers were encamped. The thud of the miners as they drove tunnels under the walls could be felt in his bed in the quiet of the night. Khalil had gathered all his great war drums to a place outside the walls known as the Accursed Tower. Their incessant beat warned the inhabitants of what to expect when the walls finally fell.

Gilbert entered Henri's chamber during the first week of May with the welcome news that King Hugh of Cyprus had arrived by sea with two thousand men, and whilst the numbers could not hope to influence the final battle, he did bring some authority to the various factions. He had attempted to arrange an armistice with the Sultan, and had sent his envoy, the Knight Templar Guillaume de Conran to convey his request. In a farcical example of the behaviour of the wilder elements of the various orders, a missile from the city had landed amongst the little party as they spoke with the Sultan. Narrowly avoiding instant execution in front of the furious Sultan, the knight was sent hurrying back to the garrison with unconditional terms of surrender. Henri grunted as he listened.

'Grand Master de Beaujeu needs to keep his Templars more in line. Does he not recognise their responsibility in arriving at this perilous stage?' he asked contemptuously, remembering his father's oft-repeated axiom that there were elements among the Templars that would rather die fighting than win any kind of lasting peace.

Gilbert nodded in agreement. Within two weeks of the attempt at diplomacy the walls around the Accursed Tower and the St Anthony's Gate were showing distinct signs of instability. Cracks had appeared, and parts of the extensive machicolations had tumbled into the streets below, as terrified citizens shrank back into their doorways.

Henri had become increasingly impatient and frustrated. The neat scab over his wound had healed, but its incessant itching was driving him mad. On the tenth day Eleanor had allowed (allowed!) him to sit a little in the sunshine in the alley way outside his quarters. She appeared regularly after sunrise to change his dressing, and smear more honey over the area. He had once protested that he saw little need in changing the dressing now that it had healed, and she had paused for a moment in her ministrations, looking at him with icy blue eyes

'If you would like to see your estates at Castres and elsewhere, my Lord, we will do it my way.'

Reflecting on this afterwards, he could not fathom why on earth he had not exploded in rage at this impertinence.

A few days after he had begun to sit in the alley, he was taking his first unaided steps. It was not as if he had broken any bones, but the violence of the surgery had made him stiffen and walk as a man twice his age. However a few circuits of the harbour area on the arm of Gilbert soon started to ease his stiffness.

The next day as Henri, Gilbert and Eleanor started their walk down to the harbour they passed the Templar Grand Master de Beaujeu. He was sitting astride his horse, urging his men on in their efforts to repair the walls with the fallen masonry. Out of a shower of arrows the Infidel had fired over the walls, a single shaft found the gap in his armour under his armpit. The three friends, watched, aghast, as the Grand Master's sword fell from his hand. His charger lurched to one side as the sword clattered onto the cobbles, and the Grand Master fell heavily to the ground. He made as if to rise then slumped back again. The soldiers, seeing their Commander fall, let out a great cry of rage and dismay.

Henri and Gilbert hurriedly ran over to the fallen Grand Master. His white cloak was now stained with his own slowly spreading blood. He looked up at the two Hospitallers. 'Gentlemen, I can do no more, look at my wound, I am dead.'

His head slumped as the two dragged him to the shelter of the stone arch. Eleanor bent over him. After a moment she glanced up at the two knights, shaking her head.

Later, as darkness fell, and in sombre mood, Henri and Gilbert climbed the narrow steps outside the makeshift hospital ward to the flat roof of the tiny stone building. As they stood, they were slightly below the level of the battlements across the narrow street, but they could see in the distance the seething mass of Khalil's army, and its gaily-coloured tents. The last rays of the dying sun caught the conical tops of the tents and illuminated them like miniature volcanoes.

Beneath the walls in front of them, and out of their sight, they could hear the raucous exchanges of the Infidel troops and the thud of the miners as they burrowed beneath the mighty walls.

To their right the Accursed Tower stood, its topmost battlements still bathed in light. As they watched, the tops of a pair of scaling ladders appeared, and three or four turbaned figures leapt over the walls. Others followed, their features dark and swarthy.

Henri and Gilbert involuntarily grasped their sword hilts, but the gap between the flat roof and the battlements was too wide. In unison they shouted to the watch on the tower, who thus far had remained ignorant of the threat beneath them in the darkness. Quickly the battlements were filled with running soldiers and the ring of clashing steel, and desperate shouts echoed across the rooftops. The garrison soon overwhelmed the little group, and the scaling ladders were pushed back to the screams of the unfortunate Infidel still scaling them.

Henri and Gilbert relaxed, and then the menacing throb of the kettledrums began again.

'They grow in confidence,' Henri said. 'Tomorrow or the next night the wall will fall...'

'We have the sea at our backs Gilbert. We should make our peace with God before we die fighting with steel in our hands.'

Gilbert nodded slowly.

'We fight for the one true God indeed, Henri, but our orders come from Pope Nicholas IV here on earth.'

Henri looked at his friend in the same manner he had during their discourse on the battlements before the abortive sortie.

Gilbert continued; 'God's fight will be won, of that there is no doubt, and we shall bring the light of His Word to the Heathen, But to that end Henri, we will need an army to defeat them.'

'Indeed my friend, but we have taken an oath, a sacred oath to defend to the death that which we hold dear.'

'And what did we do at Marqab and others?' Gilbert demanded. Henri nodded but did not reply. The pair stared out over the walls at the darkening tips of the enemy tents. Over the muted noise of the drums came a more sinister sound.

'Shields!' snapped Henri. They squatted down on the flat roof, holding their battle shields above them. Not a moment too soon. Dozens of arrows clattered onto the roof around them. Somewhere in the alley beneath them a man screamed. Henri cautiously peered round his shield and grimaced as he saw the shaft of an arrow embedded in it. Angrily he snatched it out of the leather shield, making as if to hurl it away, his eye was drawn to the discoloured tip.

'Hashashin, Gilbert. See the poison?' He pointed to the sticky residue on the arrow's tip.

The pair, holding their shields above them, made their way down the stone steps as further arrows clattered harmlessly behind them. Henri was in no doubt as to his fate should his previous captors get hold of him. He shivered involuntarily. Once in the quiet of his chamber he turned to his friend.

'So, who remains with the authority to order the Grand Masters to leave?'

Gilbert smiled, tight lipped.

'The orders are here already Henri, it's just that you haven't seen them.'

Henri shook his head annoyed, irritated.

'Orders? Orders! Gilbert, by God's word I know not of any order other than your dearest sister's orders. She treats me as a child! In God's name I swear that I am struck dumb at her words.'

Gilbert did not reply, but turned and picked up a worn leather bag from behind a curtain. Henri glimpsed manuscripts and rolls of parchment before Gilbert tied it shut. A slight noise at the door drew Henri's eyes. Eleanor stood looking at the two knights. She had changed from her light clothes and wore a dark cloak. She carried a small bag.

'We should go,' Gilbert said quietly.

CHAPTER SEVEN

The three made their way to the harbour. The streets were seething with increasingly panic-stricken inhabitants, and as they neared the port the more congested the streets became. It was late summer, and although the air was warm from the last of the sun's rays, people huddled nervously around braziers on every street corner. From the doors of taverns came the bawdy songs of Venetian and Pisan traders and sailors.

A swarthy drunken sailor, reeling from a tavern, stumbled against Eleanor. Grinning tipsily, his arm went around her. Gilbert's arm shot out of his dark cloak and with his large hand he grabbed the sailor's throat, slamming him against the wall. Terrified the sailor gasped out a choked apology. Gilbert released the man, who coughing and spluttering collapsed in the gutter.

They continued down the narrow street, the smell of the sea becoming stronger. Henri heard the running of bare feet behind them, and turned his hand on his sword. Gilbert was faster. The rasp of steel and the flash of his blade in the moonlight came as one, and the dark, rushing shape was run through. The man screamed horribly, his knife falling from his lifeless fingers as he died. Other shadowy shapes that had appeared behind him turned and fled back into the darkness.

Stooping, Gilbert wiped his blade on the man's clothing, then sheathing the sword, turned and caught up with Henri and Eleanor. Not a word was spoken. Minutes later the three reached the quayside, leaving behind them the dark confines of the narrow streets.

The port was bathed in moonlight. All the colours were grey and silver, the noise and bustle of the town faded behind them.

Already the port had almost emptied and Henri watched grimly as a galley put to sea; ships normally never sailed at night. Behind the Pisan quarter he could see the walled fortress of the Templars from which the final battle would be fought.

Eleanor moved ahead, walking briskly around the port to the outer breakwater. Here were moored *La Comptess*, and the Templar galleys *Bethania* and *Bethel*. Lines of soldiers carried crates and bundles from the lowered drawbridge of the Templar fortress to the ships. Henri noticed the distinctive bald tonsure of the Templar treasurer, Tibald de Gaudin. He was bowed over a makeshift lectern in the stern of *Bethania*, making entries in a large ledger. Already the vessel had settled substantially in the water, and it bustled with activity as the banks of oars were removed for their swivels to be greased to ensure swifter progress. Jean de Villiers, the Hospitaller Grand Master, wounded the day before, and Conrad von Feuchtwangen the Teutonic Knights Grandmaster had just been taken on board *La Comptess*, and that galley was almost ready to leave the chaos behind. The *Bethel*, was also heavily laden, but only Roger de Flor stood at the gangplank, whilst his crew laboured, stowing away the cargo.

The three friends passed the bustling *La Comptess* and *Bethania*, and Eleanor spoke as she bade Henri and Gilbert wait in the shadows of some large crates.

'When I signal, join me, but do not draw your arms.'

Henri's mouth opened but no sound came. He shook his head resignedly. 'By God, Gilbert, I would rather fight the Infidel than your sister, I swear.'

Eleanor stepped confidently across the quay to the leering Roger de Flor. Reaching him, she made a small curtsey, her voice carrying clearly over the bustle of the harbour. 'Good evening Knight de Flor. I believe you have a passage to Cyprus for sale?'

'Full, my lady, full to the gunwales, I'm afraid,' he sneeringly replied. He glanced over his shoulder to where his sailors were manoeuvring heavy crates and bundles on deck.

'I come with good authority, my lord,' Eleanor said softly and deliberately, offering her hand to him.

De Flor bent in the moonlight and straightened quickly. 'Authority without question, sister,' he frowned. 'But without gold bezants, even that is worthless.'

Henri, watching from the shadows, whispered to Gilbert. 'What has she in her hand, my friend?'

'The seal of Pope Nicholas IV, Henri,' Gilbert said, without emotion. Henri's mind reeled. This woman, sister of Gilbert, nurse to him, carrying the Papal seal?

Eleanor continued, 'I have more bezants than you can carry, but I want exclusive passage for me and my escorts.' So saying, she motioned to Henri and Gilbert, who went quickly towards her across the quay. They stood impassively either side of her diminutive figure, staring at the Templar Knight. Roger de Flor spoke contemptuously.

'A Knight of the Temple takes instruction or threat from no-one, madam. As I stated, my berths are full, and we sail tomorrow. My passengers have delivered to me their valuables.' He paused, motioning towards the galley. 'We shall sail on the morning tide, unless of course those Infidel dogs get here before that.' He cocked his head at the low, incessant murmur of the drums.

Eleanor's tone hardened. 'Sir, you do recognise the seal? Refusal can be construed as treason…even heresy. We are on Papal business under direct orders of Pope Nicholas IV. We carry documents that must not fall into Sultan Khalil's hands—'

'I care not for your seal, lady; I have a full complement of generous, fare-paying lady passengers. Now if you will excuse me…'

Gilbert and Henri exchanged a glance above Eleanor's head. Swift as the gesture was, it was enough to cause de Flor's hand to fly to his sword hilt. Before the two Knights could react, Eleanor's own hand appeared from under her cloak, going swiftly for the Knight's throat. His eyes bulged. Then a thin trickle of dark scarlet ran down Eleanor's pale, slim hand. De Flor slid to the ground without a sound. Eleanor stood, the moonlight gleaming wetly on the long slim blade in her hand. De Flor's eyes rolled upwards and he fell backwards. There was a barely discernible splash in the dark waters between the boat and the quay. The weight of his armour carried him swiftly beneath the dark surface. Eleanor, breathing hard, turned to her brother, her eyes glittering,

'Take over command Gilbert, double the crew's rates. We sail for Narbonne on the morning tide.'

So saying, she took Henri's arm and led him unresistingly along the quay to the Temple Gate. The speed at which Eleanor had dispatched de Flor would have impressed even the trained killers of the Hashashin, Henri mused. He also realised that his reluctantly growing admiration for Eleanor de Gothia was tempered by the possibility that one wrong move on his part could well prove fatal.

Eleanor continued conversationally, as if the incident had not occurred, 'You lost your father to the Infidel, I believe?'

She paused, and Henri spoke forcefully, his feelings high, 'And my brothers and my mother.' He stopped suddenly. 'And you wish me to flee now?' he asked her.

'Not flee my lord, no, not flee. Rather to lead the fight for the one True God from elsewhere'. She held out the Great Seal of the Pope, the bronze key of St Peter embossed with Nicholas's IV insignia. 'Our presence here is no accident'. She gestured back to the boat where Gilbert was watching. 'Neither is yours'. She looked directly at him with cool blue eyes. 'Our late friend de Flor has accumulated a King's ransom, but Gilbert has a document that dwarfs even that.' She smiled, thin lipped and pale, at Henri.

'The Templar ship, *Bethel*, looks as heavily laden as the *Bethania*,' she continued, 'This new Grand Master, the one who'll be sworn in following William de Beaujeu's death—what is his name?'

'Tibald, Tibald de Gaudin, their treasurer,' offered Henri.

'That's his standard flying on the *Bethania*,' she rejoined. 'He's ready to leave with the Templar coffers, its only good fortune that Khalil's Egyptian friends have not sailed into Acre. If they do…'

Henri saw at once the opportunity to acquire another vessel laden with treasure.

'If I can persuade Tibald to sail early, we would have two valuable vessels on the high seas.' He paused uncertainly.

Eleanor spoke softly, 'Vessels that contain the remnants of the Christian wealth which we can use to continue the fight.' Henri noticed her use of the plural and increased his pace as they entered the Temple courtyard.

'I believe Tibald de Gaudin knew my mother...' he murmured.

Eleanor watched him approach a portly tonsured figure holding court amongst a group of Knights.

Previously the Treasurer of the Knights Templar, de Gaudin had just been elected Grand Master on the death of Beaujeu. Eleanor gave a faint smile of approval. If anybody knew what treasures to load aboard the three vessels, Tibald de Gaudin did. Watching, she saw him bow his head as Henri spoke softly into his ear.

Dawn streaked the pale blue sky, and the tempo and volume of the rumbling kettledrums increased. The loading of the vessels had continued throughout the night, and they lay with sails loosely furled, ready to leave at a moment's notice.

Henri and Gilbert had returned in the small hours to St Anthony's Gate. Though Henri accepted the authority of the Great Seal, he was still reluctant to be leaving. He wrestled with his conscience, memories of his father, mother and brothers drifting through his mind. Were they calling him to fight and remain in the Holy Land, or was a higher authority calling him on? He shook his head as if to clear it.

The pair stood on the battlements looking along their length. Even in what remained of the darkness they could see jagged gaps in the wall. As they watched, the ground outside the City seemed to ferment and seethe, as the approaching dawn signalled, hundreds of Infidel soldiers beginning to pace menacingly towards the walls.

The drumbeats increased their rhythm—and then Khalil's war trumpets began their strident notes. Henri glanced quickly at Gilbert. Grim faced the other man nodded. Down in the harbour the early rays of sunshine had yet to reach the calm waters, yet they could see the two vessels being pulled along the breakwater. The lead vessel, the *Bethania*, carrying the Templar Grand Master unfurled its snowy white mizzen sail, the blood red Templar cross billowing bravely as it caught an offshore breeze. Slowly the first vessel cleared the breakwater. As one, the pair turned and ran down the narrow steps from the battlements. Hastening down the still darkened streets, their mantles flowed behind them; their boots rang on the cobbles. As they entered the harbour, they saw *Bethel* was nearing the end of the breakwater.

'Quickly!' Henri shouted as they hurtled along the quayside. Breathing hard, they leapt the widening gulf between the *Bethel* and the quay as she followed *Bethania* out of the harbour.

Eleanor, already on board, flashed them a furious look for their tardiness. The *Bethel*, heavily laden as she was, had, of course, sailed without her compliment of paying passengers. Nevertheless a dozen of Gilbert's knights lay gratefully on the bulging cargo more than a little relieved to have survived thus far.

'I though it best to bring an exchange crew, Henri, should we have to run more than one galley,' Gilbert said.

'I wasn't aware you spoke for your sister,' Henri replied teasing his friend, watching Eleanor give directions to the coxswain to follow the wake of the *Bethania*.

Eleanor finished issuing her orders and joined the two men on the forepeak.

'King Hugh de Lusignon of Cyprus is with de Villiers on *La Comptess*' she said. 'That means Cyprus is our first port of call. We should await developments there, I think.'

The three vessels made steady progress away from the rising sun. Shading their eyes against its fiery brightness, only the outline of Acre could be seen, but already several plumes of smoke were climbing into the blue morning sky. Henri stood with Gilbert and Eleanor on the gently heaving deck of the *Bethel*. For a long time they stood in silence.

At last Henri spoke. 'Let us not in this hour of defeat harbour a single thought that this is the end. Rather say that this is the beginning of the end for the Infidel across the world. Urban II's call will be honoured, if it takes until the end of time.'

Somewhere amongst the gaily-coloured tents, under the crumbling walls of Acre, an obscure Arab historian was penning his memoirs:

'With these conquests, all the lands of the coast were fully returned to the children of Allah. Thus were the Franks expelled from all the lands of Syria. May the Prophet grant that they never set foot here again.'

CHAPTER EIGHT

The three vessels cleared the coast and turned towards Tyre and Sidon, these being the next two strongholds rumoured still to be in Christian hands. Little was said as the galleys slipped northwards in the calm waters. On the shore a cloud of dust rising from a group of galloping horsemen kept pace with them. For four days this strange parallel race continued, the ships not needing to weigh anchor at night, since there was a full moon to navigate by. The Captain of *La Comptess*, unwilling to contemplate that the entire coast was now hostile, made to turn into the Port of Tyre—surely a safe haven, held, as it was by Almaric, King Hugh of Cyprus's brother. As they approached the harbour a small vessel was leaving, flying the Red Lion, the Cypriot flag. Henri and Eleanor, from the deck of the *Bethel*, offshore and a short distance away, could not hear the shouted warnings between the crews of the two vessels but as the Cypriot vessel continued to sea, *La Comptess* performed a graceful arc in the mouth of the River Litani and continued north in the wake of the *Bethania*. As the vessels regained their close formation, it became clear just how near they had come to sailing their treasures into the hands of the Infidel. Tyre had been surrendered without a fight to Khalil's Emir, Shujai.

The little flotilla continued north, still accompanied by the dust cloud of galloping horsemen on the shore. As darkness fell the three vessels moored at the last outpost of the coast, the Castle of the Sea at Sidon.

Aptly named it stood on a small rocky island that allowed immunity from the pursuing horsemen on the shore. For the first time in a week, the ship's companies disembarked and ate frugally at the castle. It was a sombre affair. Tibald, now Grand Master of not very much, was painfully aware he was fleeing the Holy Land. He sought out Henri, who listened politely, offering little comment. It was decided the Castle be abandoned before Shujai's engineers completed the causeway they were constructing from the beach. Putting on a confident air, Tibald declared the fight for the Holy Land would continue from Cyprus under the protection of King Hugh. There at last the Templars could regroup, lick their wounds, and beg further funds from the Pope for a new and greater crusade.

At dawn the following day, the three vessels set sail for Cyprus. The two Knights stood close together, watching the land they had fought for so desperately slip away from them. Each felt an almost unbearable sense of loss; of something integral having gone from their lives, and which perhaps would never return.

For Henri, a pall seemed to settle over the ship as the true nature of their situation became clear to him. Bound for Europe, a place of which he knew little, not only with Gilbert, but also with Eleanor, who was beginning to fill more and more of his thoughts. It was his growing uncertainty about what lay ahead that finally drove him to question Gilbert directly about his mysterious Order, the Anthonines.

He already knew a little of their history from the discussions back in Acre. Strange though it seemed, although the Order came under the jurisdiction of the Hospitallers, each Order maintained a large degree of secrecy from the others, in the same way that the Order of Notre Dame de Sion did under the Templars. Henri, inheriting his late father's contempt of the posturing Templars, had, under his mother's insistence, once he had returned from the Hashashins, joined the Hospitallers. This was originally a monastic nursing order, founded by the Blessed Gerard, and confirmed by a Papal Bull of Pope Paschal II in 1113. Their origins stretched back to 600 AD, when Abbot Probus had been commissioned by Pope Gregory the Great to build a hostel in Jerusalem to treat and care for Christian Pilgrims to the Holy Land. It was subsequently destroyed by Caliph el Hakim, and then rebuilt in 1023 by merchants from Amalfi and Salerno, by permission of Caliph Haroun el Rashid of

Egypt. From their origins of caring for the sick pilgrims, they soon expanded into providing armed escorts, due to the rapidly growing tensions between Islam and the Christian world. By Henri's time most of the actual nursing had been delegated to the Benedictine monks, as the Hospitallers developed into a smaller, more compact version of their brothers, the Knights Templar.

Gilbert and Eleanor had looked at each other with a strange half smile at Henri's questions.

'Our line stretches back nearly one thousand years,' began Gilbert. 'St Anthony was the first monk to attempt to codify our existence in pursuit of the Kingdom of God. He was a hermit who lived by the Red Sea, and he died on January 17th 356.'

Gilbert paused, glancing at Eleanor. She continued, her eyes shining, 'The Knights of St Anthony is the oldest Chivalric Order in the world, and was officially formed as part of the defence of the Christian King Prester John in Ethiopia. However our own legend has it that the original Knights came from a troop of nine of the Roman Emperor Constantine's 'Golden Knights' who were sent to Egypt to bring St Anthony to Rome to meet Constantine in 322. But that when Anthony The Hermit refused to go to Rome they stayed and were taught by him, and that at his death they went to Ethiopia to aid Prester John, calling themselves Knights of The Order of St Anthony the Hermit.'

'There were also nine Knights of St Anthony at the Battle of Poitiers in 732 with Charles Martell. In 1095 they formed close links with the Pope, and founded the Hospitaller Order of St Anthony'

'Wasn't that the date of the Council of Clermont, in which Urban II started the Crusades?' interjected Henri, not wishing to be left behind in this sudden excursion into intellectual discussion.

Eleanor nodded, smiling slightly. The wind had risen and the rhythmic slap of the waves had taken a deeper resonance.

'The founder of our Hospitaller Order, Gaston de Dauphine, who was an Anthonine, had a son who fell ill in 1095, and he was praying before the relics of St Anthony in the Church of St Didier la Mothe, near Vienne, when he had a vision of how to cure his son's illness. Several weeks previously a number of his villagers had fallen to the same disease afflicting his son.'

'First of all they scratched themselves so hard their fingernails drew blood. Then they went berserk and ran screaming around the village, yelling and shouting that they felt as if they were on fire. All the while their eyes rolled until just the whites were visible and they frothed at the mouth. Within a day, their hands and feet began to turn grey, then black, as the flesh rotted. Infection set in and raced to the centre of the body. Even so, death took many days. The poor wretches kept up their screaming and writhing until the last'.

Eleanor fell silent. All were aware of the dreaded disease that afflicted young and old alike. Sometimes, and no one knew why, limbs merely withered away, and the victim became a leper, outcast from society, condemned to a living death.

Gilbert continued, 'Gaston saw in a dream a concoction he needed to defeat the disease, which later became known as St Anthony's Fire. When this succeeded in curing his son, he went to Clermont to offer his life to God and the Crusades. He met Clement V, who persuaded him to write his remedies down and continue his work in France. During his work, Gaston also discovered what caused the disease as well as how to cure it.'

Gilbert paused and glanced at Henri, who was watching his friend with a newfound respect. He had not realised that his comrade in arms of the last six years was so erudite.

Eleanor continued smoothly, 'We, that is, the Anthonines, then had the power of both creating and curing the disease, which gave us the freedom to roam Europe, curing doomed people. Gaston's book of remedies was then brought to the Holy Land, where it was used by our Order in their hospitals.'

She paused, glancing towards Gilbert.

'You mean that was what Gilbert was looking for?' asked Henri.

Eleanor nodded, 'The book was lost to the Order during the earlier crusades, and it is only through Gilbert's diligence that its whereabouts was discovered.'

Now our Order's Knights and Hospitallers have Preceptories throughout France, and other lands. We are heading back to one of our nine Preceptories at Rhedae in Septimania, which is not far from your estate at Castres.'

'I should also tell you that our Order differs from other orders in that our members do not take vows of poverty or chastity but only holy obedience to our Grand Prior. In fact we encourage marriage between members of our order and our children inherit their parent's obligations. Our own family and the families of our Commanders trace an unbroken line from the original nine Golden Knights of Constantine.'

The conversation lapsed as one of Gilbert's men brought around coarse bread, olives and a small flagon of wine each. The waves had eased a little and the sun glittered off a brilliant blue sea. Henri got to his feet and paced along the deck. They were completely out of sight of land. Uneasy, he sank down again on the deck. Eleanor watched him as he ate. From time to time she licked a crumb from her lips, took a sip of wine. After a while both she and Gilbert, having finished their meal, rose, and smiling at Henri, left him to his thoughts.

It was as the sun was setting that Henri sought them out, wrapping his cloak about him against the evening chill.

'We sail from the land of our God after being soundly defeated by the Infidel hordes. All our lives we have fought and plotted and planned for the return of Jerusalem to the one True Faith, and for nought. As if our God has forsaken us, we are cast out upon the ocean, whilst hordes of filthy unbelievers run rampage over our sacred land.' He spoke in bitterness and in deep anger.

'And yet, and yet,' he continued softly, 'we flee in ships containing fabulous wealth. And now we have, if you are to be believed,' he looked hard at Eleanor, 'a book giving us power to create and cure disease; the power of life and death.'

He paused. Gilbert and Eleanor gazed at him. They did not speak, but Eleanor's eyes shone in the approaching dusk.

Henri continued softly. 'We would not be the first in history to be fleeing our Holy Land, nor the first to be carrying great wealth and knowledge. I only can hope and pray that somehow this situation in which we find ourselves will enable us to acquit ourselves with honour.'

Now, far from the warmth of the land, the westerly breeze propelling them towards Cyprus had developed a definite chill, and the three huddled on the open forepeak of the *Bethel*, the only one of the three ships not to have an enclosed cabin. And in spite of his solemn vows Henri could not but be aware of the small heat Eleanor's body generated. Eventually, after much deliberation, he rested his arm around her shoulder and she snuggled back into his arms as they slept.

On the fifth day the low mountainous bulk of Cyprus came into view, and on the evening of that day the two vessels, *Bethania* and *Bethel*, slipped into Larnaca Bay to dock at Skala, where *La Comptess* was already moored. The Templars had an interest in the Island of Cyprus, on which, although they had sold the bulk of it to King Hugh, they still maintained a healthy presence.

Within the sheltering arms of the bay, and with the backdrop of the dun-coloured mountains, the waters were as smooth as glass. For the first time in many days the motion of the boat stabilised somewhat. The *Bethania* and *Bethel* headed for the harbour behind the long stone breakwater. Gilbert's troops became boisterous and loud in anticipation of being on dry land. These were not seasoned sailors, and the constant motion at sea had caused much sickness.

The vessels dropped their sails, whilst the crew manoeuvred the boats alongside the quay using the oars. Henri was first off and he leapt the narrowing gap with ease. He was a little unsteady as he stood on the stone quay, swaying, with his arms outstretched as he attempted to regain his balance after days of pitching and rolling at sea.

Gilbert likewise landed on the dock, and weaved unsteadily towards the large stone bollards by which the ships were moored. To much muttered protest, Henry and Gilbert gave orders that the ships be turned around with their bows to sea. Only when the sails had been furled correctly and the little ships made ready for sea again did Henri pay off the crew, warning them to stay close to the harbour.

When they were satisfied that the vessels were secure, Henri, Gilbert and Eleanor made their way to the cluster of taverns and stores lining the rear of the harbour. From one of the narrow streets shouts and laughter could be heard, accompanied by feminine screams. The sun shone and the air was warm and still. Henri, walking on the edge of the quay, could see into the clear blue waters where fish of many brilliant colours swam and darted amongst the little fishing boats. He felt an immense sensation of relief and wellbeing flow through his body. His eyes took in the pretty, peaceful harbour; he savoured the smells of cooking, the relaxed air of the port. For the first time in his life the Infidel were just distant memories. He welcomed this feeling—it was one of hope and of a growing confidence in the future.

He glanced behind to where Eleanor was strolling arm-in-arm with Gilbert. She was conversing earnestly with him, but she smiled at Henri, her eyes sparkling. Henri filled his lungs with the sweet salty air and strode ahead to the Tavern.

CHAPTER NINE

It was not long after their arrival that Tibald de Gaudin hastened to consult with Jean de Villiers, Grand Master of the Hospitallers, who had arrived on board the Hospitaller's flagship *La Comptess* and was Henri's direct superior. The two Grand Masters accompanied by Henri and Gilbert talked long into the night. It was evident that the sensitive political situation of the island Kingdom precluded a long stay there. Jean decided at last that the best course for the Hospitallers was to attempt to secure the Island of Rhodes upon which a long lasting and secure base could be built, leaving Cyprus for the Templars and King Hugh to squabble over.

Gilbert and Henri spent the next few days on horseback exploring the lush island. However, unbeknown to Henri, every evening Gilbert and Eleanor would spend hours alone poring over the Book that they had brought with them from the Holy Land. After several days Gilbert disappeared into the cellar of their quarters and returned with shallow trays covered in damp cloths. These were filled with mouldering rye seeds, which Gilbert turned over gently with a small wooden paddle, before returning them to the cellar. Later, he dried them, and then ground the mouldy seeds into flour, before preparing a number of small, unleavened cakes.

Eleanor took a batch of these to Tibald de Gaudin's court during her ministrations to a sick soldier. Tibald had been in a black depression since arriving in Cyprus. The loss of the Holy Land had weighed heavily on him. In spite of his vow to return to Sidon with a Templar army, he had not been able to do so.

Within several days of Eleanor's visit, rumours swept the Island of Tibald's strange behaviour. First he had spent some days furiously scratching himself. After that he had complained that his skin felt as if it was burning, and in obvious distress, he had taken to dousing himself continuously with cold water. King Hugh, fearfully hearing of the presence of the dreaded St Anthony's Fire on his island, confined himself to the mountain-top fortress, leaving the *Bethania* in the harbour under the guard of a dozen men.

Gilbert took himself to the quayside and gathered his men around him on the *Bethel*. Ribald shouts and laughter drifted across from the *Bethania* as the crew, taking full advantage of their lack of leadership, cavorted drunkenly with the harlots of the port. Gilbert left shortly afterwards, and whilst some of his men quietly continued with preparing the *Bethel*, others collected fist-sized pebbles from the seabed.

Later in the day, nobody took any notice of the cloaked and hooded woman as she walked the quay with a basked of freshly baked loaves. A sergeant-of-arms, lolling against the hawsers of the *Bethania*, hailed her, looking hungrily at her and her basket of bread. Eleanor's tones, rebuking the leering drunken sergeant as he purchased the entire basket for his men, could be heard across the harbour.

✠✠✠

Jean de Villiers, an old friend of Henri's as well as his master looked down at the kneeling figure before him. Sir Henri de Montfort would indeed be a great loss to the Hospitallers, as well as to any future Crusade. Guillaume attempted to remonstrate with him.

'Your family, Henri…' he said. 'You have lost much, but to leave the Order now would surely be a grave mistake for you and a great loss to us.'

Henri nodded, 'I cannot serve both you and my heart Master, and I will not break my vows. I beg you release me from them so I may at last try to follow my true feelings for the Lady Eleanor de Gothia.'

There was no doubt that the union of the de Montfort and de Gothia families would be a mighty force working for the one true

God, of that much he was sure. Guillaume hoped that Henri's strong resolve and clarity of purpose, joined to Eleanor's wealth would lead on to greater triumphs for the Holy Church.

With a heavy heart, Guillame formally agreed to Henri's request that he be released from his vows of chastity as a Knight Hospitaller. Inclining his head, he reluctantly gave his blessing.

✠✠✠

The entire troop guarding the *Bethania* had succumbed to the same illness as Tibald de Gaudin. They lay on rough palliasses around the harbour, thrashing and moaning, whilst pouring seawater over themselves. The salt water on the fresh scratches made them howl even more. The more fortunate inhabitants of the harbour buildings had fled up to the hills in an attempt to avoid the fate of the soldiers.

Gilbert went down to the *Bethel* in the harbour, with its rigging slack and the sails furled. He took an iron marlin spike from its housing on the gunwales and gave it to one of his troop. Rapidly he passed round another half a dozen of the wicked-looking spikes, bidding his men follow him along the quay. Jumping down into one of King Hugh's galleys, he placed the tip of the spike on the bottom of the hull. After striking the top of it sharply with the fist-sized stone he wrenched it out of the wood to be rewarded by the gurgle of water. He returned to the quay. The whole process had taken less than a minute. He motioned his men to do likewise to the other vessels.

The next day Jean de Villiers stood gazing out at a harbour appallingly empty of vessels. Empty, that is, of floating ships, for under the gently swelling surface the outline of the galleys could be seen, their masts and rigging giving the harbour the somewhat surreal look of an exotic reed bed, only his own ship *La Comptess* remained intact Of the two vessels, *Bethania* and *Bethel* there was no sign.

The harbour remained inaccessible for some time whilst the afflicted soldiers recovered, and it was a little while before King

Hugh ventured from his eyrie to view his sunken fleet. The monarch ranted furiously from his mountain fortress, for the *Bethania* contained a goodly portion of the Cypriot King's wealth. He also vented considerable anger on the two possible successors to the late Tibald de Gaudin, one Hugh de Peraud, the Templar Treasurer, and another Knight, Jacques de Molay, proven in the battlefield and Master of the Templars in England, who would eventually become the next Grand Master of The Temple.

Whilst the two protagonists argued and discussed the rift between the Templars and the Hospitallers, a debate that was going to take the best part of a year, the two galleys, the *Bethel* and the *Bethania* slipped silently westwards, followed the next day by *La Comptess* with Grand Master Jean de Villiers on board on his way to Rhodes.

✠✠✠

A journey of almost two thousand miles lay ahead of them and Henri was now under no illusion as to the ruthlessness of his companions or the hazards and dangers facing them. Whilst their vessels were arguably the finest in the Templar fleet, they were also heavily laden and severely under-crewed. Henri had no experience of sea warfare, but during his time on Cyprus he had heard enough about the Sicilian pirates to know that the narrowing of the ocean in between Sicily and the North African coast could be very dangerous. But with the promise of a little gold and a lot more on their safe arrival at Narbonne, the services of a dozen Cypriot bowmen had been acquired before they had embarked. Their short stubby bows would be issued in time of need, and a prodigious supply of arrows was held on each boat. Remembering the actions of Kala'un's miners, several earthenware urns containing flammable naptha from Asia had also been procured.

As the two ships headed ever westward towards Narbonne, Henri found himself gazing more and more often at Eleanor. When on occasion she happened to notice this, she returned his look with complete equanimity, her cool blue eyes giving little away.

Once a long, long time ago, he had hunted in the mountains of Armenia on his mother's family estates, and after a particularly long and arduous climb at the end of which he found himself quite alone, he had rounded a rocky outcrop to find himself face to face with a mountain leopard.

He was so close he could smell the rank animal odour. Henri had frozen to the spot as, tail lashing ominously, the cat's great yellow eyes blazed into his. Then with an explosive grunt the animal had leapt from the path in front of him and away down the cliff. Henri had no doubt at all that the cat's decision not to kill him was hers and hers alone. Disturbingly he brought the little scene from his past to the fore whenever Eleanor regarded him. He was also reminded of the ease with which Roger de Flor had been dispatched back in Acre. He couldn't quite bring himself to admit it, but he did harbour the suspicion that in some strange way his destiny had already chosen.

Henri did not object to this, but he became puzzled and not a little envious when some of the looks she shot him were preceded or followed by a long discussion with Gilbert. Try as he might, he could not persuade his friends to share the contents of their discussions, and he was feeling isolated and left out, which as a commander he was unused to.

From Cyprus their natural route would have led them onto the island of Rhodes, but having knowledge of Guillaume de Villaret's plans for the Hospitallers to take over the island, and bearing in mind the value of the two vessels cargo, they avoided the island and sailed straight for Crete. Here they berthed at the end of the breakwater, as far away from the centre of the harbour as possible, to ensure a rapid and unimpeded departure. Gilbert, having divided the crews up more evenly, had moved to the *Bethel*, leaving Henri the sole use of the luxurious aft cabin of the *Bethania*. Without allowing the crews to rest, orders were given to re-victual and replenish the water supplies aboard the vessels. Only after this was accomplished to Gilbert's satisfaction did he allow the crews to head towards the taverns of the harbour. They would need all their strength and resolve for the passage ahead.

Henri had never learnt to swim. All his life had been spent in dry, gritty conditions, where the provision of water in any quantity was deemed a privilege of the rich. During the years of his captivity by the Hashashin his one recurring dream had been of the maids fetching warmed water from the kitchen fire to fill his bath at his father's castle. It was therefore with some fascination that he watched Eleanor, after Gilbert had released the crew onshore, remove her outer garments and wearing simply a cotton shift, dive gleefully from the deck into the warm blue sea. He was even more amazed to watch her swim and splash confidently around the schools of cavorting dolphins that accompanied them from time to time and were gathered around the harbour entrance. One day she had cajoled him to join her in the water Her floating cotton shift held a fascination he could not quite erase from his mind. The diaphanous display of long legs beneath the flimsy material became too much for him. With an oath he stripped his soiled, sweat-soaked garments from his body and vaulted onto the wide rail around the stern of the vessel. Eleanor squealed and covered her eyes as her laughter rang out. Henri paused, balanced precariously on the rail, his muscular figure showing not an ounce of spare flesh. He glanced around. It was midday, and the port slumbered under the hot sun. The harbour was deserted.

It occurred to Henri as he stepped into thin air that perhaps he should have taken some lessons in the art of swimming, but it was too late. He landed with an almighty splash next to a shrieking Eleanor. He had barely taken in her wet laughing face when the green waters closed above him. He had no difficulty in opening his eyes in the clean, warm aquamarine sea as his jump carried him deep beneath her. Glancing upwards towards the light he saw instantly her slim star shaped figure silhouetted against the sunlit waves. For a moment he was spellbound, then the pressure on his lungs became too great and with rising panic he lashed out at his watery prison. As he watched the silvery surface draw nearer, his lungs felt as if they would explode, and he burst from the water gulping great quantities of clean fresh air. Eleanor's peals of laughter rang around him, and he had barely chance to catch his breath, before he felt long smooth legs grip him in a scissor movement. Even in his perilous state his mind registered the thick curly bush of hair in the fork of her legs as she momentarily held his torso in her grip. Then he was under again. This time when he surfaced, mucus and water streaming from his mouth, he weakly paddled to the sides of the *Bethania*.

Later, as the sun touched the blackening sea, he sat in his aft cabin. The door opened confidently, and Eleanor entered. She had dried and brushed her curly titian locks, and the shift she was wearing floated around her body. The last rays of sunlight danced in her hair briefly as she closed the door. Henri stood, uncertain for a moment. She drew close to him. Her warm, feminine odour assailed him, and the drawstring around her shoulders holding up her white cotton shift held a fascination all of its own. He made to speak, but with a small shake of her head she picked up his hand, brushed it across her lips and put it on the drawstring.

✠✠✠

Dawn several days later found them in between the coast of Tunisia and the distant mountains of Sicily. For the first time in weeks the westerly wind deserted them, and they made slow heading with the oars in the still, oily sea. Just before the sun reached its zenith Henri, hearing Gilbert's warning shout, looked up quickly. Two vessels were approaching with a considerable degree of speed.

Gilbert shouted to Henri to hoist, 'Le Drapeau Jolie Rouge.' This little red flag emblazoned with a white scull and crossed leg bones was the feared battle flag of the Templar fleet, and Gilbert hoped that the sight of it may deter the approaching corsair raiders. Putting every available man on the oars, the two Knights began issuing bows to the bowmen. A pot of naptha was given to each man and, after much coaxing from the supply of tinder, a small guttering candle. The corsair vessels had an edge on speed owing to their double-banked oars, but Henri and Gilbert turned and aimed their vessels straight at the oncoming ships. The corsairs' tactics were to ram a vessel broadside on, and using the weight of the fast moving boat, push the victim's ship under the surface. Henri's plan demanded that they aim straight for the pirates head on, and at the last possible moment before a collision, pass closely down one side of the pirate vessel.

Closer, closer the vessels drew. Henri could not tear his eyes away, but he knew Gilbert watched closely on his port side.

'Hard to port!' he bellowed, fearing he had left it too late. The bow of the *Bethania* veered slowly to the left, and the pirate vessel appeared on the starboard quarter not ten yards away.

'Starboard oars in!' he shouted. His oarsmen pulled their dripping blades into the vessel. The bow of the *Bethania* ploughed into the double bank of the pirates' oars, snapping them off like matchsticks, or forcing the long wooden shafts into the oarsmen's bodies, to screams of agony. Simultaneously the Cypriot bowmen stood up and rapidly poured arrow after arrow tipped with flaming naptha into the corsair ships. In minutes it was all over. The two ships combined closing speeds caused them to pass each other rapidly, and while the *Bethania* redeployed its starboard oars, she and the *Bethel* continued westward. Behind them the corsairs had slewed around and lay dead in the water, whilst their devastated crews were torn between attempting to redistribute their remaining oars or put out the rapidly escalating fires beneath the decks. As the screams of agony and outrage drifted steadily astern, the flames took hold, and presently all that remained behind were two fiercely burning ships.

CHAPTER TEN

The cold winter sun streaming through the windows of the Benedictine Abbey of St Benoit's in Castres lifted Henri's heart. All the same he still shivered in the chill of the monastery. He found his thoughts drifting back to all that had happened. Lately he had to fight at times to remember that his first thirty-four years of life had been spent in an almost constant struggle against heat and dust and lack of clean water; to recall the battles he had fought and the friends and family he had lost.

From the moment the two vessels had left the sweltering coast of Outremer seven months previously, it was as if a shutter had descended on that part of his life. He had of course been with Gilbert de Gothia since Marqab in 1285, and the two had become as close as brothers. And then Eleanor had come along, fitting so neatly, dovetailing into his life and thoughts.

They had landed at Narbonne in the late summer. The two Templar galleys now flying the Blue Tau cross flag of the Order of St Anthony, had attracted some local interest, but the sudden appearance of a group of particularly burly monks had fended off the townsfolk's attention. Smitten with Eleanor, Henri had paid scant attention to the rapid unloading of the vessel's cargo onto a convoy of some thirteen ox carts that appeared on the quayside.

Henri had spoken volubly regarding his estates at Castres and l'Amaury near Paris, as if he were somehow seeking to impress the titian-haired beauty at his side. Suddenly and without warning he understood the attraction of spending his life with Eleanor, and to enjoy with her both his estates, neither of which he had ever seen.

Located about three days' ride from Narbonne along the river Agout, the old fortified town of Castres clustered around the ancient Abbey of St Benoit, in which he now stood. His titles of Lord of Castres and of l'Amaury near Paris had not, in truth, meant a lot to him during his life in the Holy Land, but since his arrival in the Languedoc his memories of his father's journeys through his estates in Tyre came flooding back. As a small boy he had derived childlike pleasure watching the local population treat his father with deference and respect. Now as he rode through his ancestral lands he sat a little higher in the saddle, and looked forward in anticipation of showing his estates to Eleanor. He had given scant thought as to the location of the actual estate, and so was forced to ask for directions.

Hailing a small group of shabbily dressed men on the side of the track, he called, 'Good day, I am Henri de Montfort, Lord of Castres. Have the goodness to direct me to my estate.'

Used as he was to a certain level of servility, the dark looks and mutterings of the first group took him a little by surprise. A negative answer of sorts forced him to ask a second group further down the track, and a third. After each enquiry the result was the same, and he found to his chagrin a rising sense of fury and bitterness at this unexpected atmosphere of rebellious rudeness. Two or three scowling individuals had even hawked and spat in the mud beneath his horse's hooves, scuttling away into the dense woods as he uttered an oath and made to draw his sword. Their disturbance of the undergrowth had startled a small flock of birds, which in turn made Henri's horse prance and circle in the middle of the track. Exploding with rage Henri drew his sword with a shout and gathering his horse's reins made to dash into the forest in pursuit of the insolent group. Before he could do so he felt a firm grip on his arm. Eleanor was regarding him with cool blue eyes. She said nothing but raised her hand placatingly. Henri returned her gaze unsure as to why he had halted his headlong rush into the undergrowth. After a moment Eleanor dismounted and approached a group of women who had been observing the little scene. She soon discovered the reason behind the resentment of the populace.

The town remembered with anguish the Albigensian Crusades against the Cathars some ninety years previously, in which Catholic was set against Catholic on the direct orders of Pope Innocent III. The commander of the Papal Legate charged with destroying the heretics was Arnold Amalaricus, and in turn one of his more enthusiastic generals, and proponent of the Pope's wishes was Simon de Mountford, Henri's great uncle.

Encouraged by the Papal promise of land which included Castres in return for crushing the Cathar population, and accompanied by his Dominican Inquisitors, he had watched as the heretics were burnt at the stake, proclaiming arrogantly in the nearby town of Beziers, as over one thousand Catholics were herded together in the church of St Nazaire, 'Kill them all. God will know His own,' as he set fire to the building, and the de Montfort name was still accursed in this part of France..

Eleanor thanked the group of women politely, and remounted her horse. She took the lead and cantered off down the track, followed by Henri. After several turns and a steep climb the two of them emerged from the forest and found a large fortified house built on the edge of a precipice. Surrounding the house was a substantial stone wall with a huge wooden gate. The gate leant drunkenly against the pillar, and through it Henri and Eleanor could see an overgrown track leading to the house, which was slightly raised above the level of the surrounding land. Henri reined in his horse.

'My grandfather Guy de Montfort left this place fifty years ago,' he said. He dismounted, bidding Eleanor to do likewise. The two picked their way through the remains of the gate and struggled through the waist high weeds to the front of the house. The huge wooden door, battered and scarred, resisted all attempts to force an entrance. Henri circled the great house, to no avail. All the entrances were boarded up, and had obviously not been disturbed for many years. He sat down on a fallen tree trunk as Eleanor joined him. He had not given much thought as to what this moment would bring, but now, faced with the cold reality of his homecoming, he was momentarily overcome by despair.

In the distance the sight of the snow-covered Pyrenees under a leaden sky sent a shiver down his back. He got up after a while and, followed by Eleanor, walked slowly to where his horse was tethered. The pair headed back to the town and the comfortable quarters of the Abbey.

He had looked forward so much to showing Eleanor the house where she would soon be mistress. Waiting now at the altar of the Abbey, where she was about to become his bride, he resolved firmly to overcome his sense of betrayal and disillusion. They were young. The future, with all its promise, lay ahead of them. He turned at the peal of trumpets to see his bride approaching slowly. Briefly the sun illuminated her face as it shone in between the mighty pillars of the Church. She smiled radiantly back at him. On her right, linking her arm walked a burly figure. His usual tonsure was covered by his bishop's mitre, and the cross on his staff glinted in the sunlight as the couple made their way towards Henri.

The Bishop of Bordeaux, Bertrand de Gothia, regarded Henri impassively, acknowledging by the merest inclination of his head the man who was to become the husband of his niece Eleanor de Gothia.

Henri had met Bertrand a week or so after their arrival at Castres, when he and Eleanor had visited him at the Gothia family estate at Villandraut. Putting aside his bitter anger at the condition of his own estates, Henri had rapidly realised that if, as he had long suspected, Gilbert and Eleanor were driven by some strange, secret purpose, then the catalyst was Bertrand de Gothia. Theoretically Bishop of Bordeaux, which at this time was an English dominion, his influence extended to the Papal court and the group of cardinals who, due to the Pope's illness, were now jostling for position. Henri had no knowledge of the machinations of the Papal court, but usually when he had entered a room Bertrand, Eleanor and Gilbert had been in deep discussion, as often as not with of a couple of the Anthonine monks wearing their Tau crosses. He had questioned both Eleanor and Gilbert independently as to the whereabouts of the *Bethania's* and *Bethel's* cargo but had received little intelligence.

He was no fool and resolved to put the question off until after the wedding on the seventeenth of January. The date itself meant little to him, chosen as it was by Eleanor, until he realised that it was the feast of St Anthony, and that the entire Abbey's complement of Anthonine monks would be present for the ceremony. Again, although he perhaps thought he should, he did not object or question this, but felt drawn by currents stronger than his own will. Having been bitterly disappointed by the condition of his estates in Castres, he had taken the step of sending a party of monks, chosen by Gilbert, to l'Amaury on the outskirts of Paris. If he were to make a home in that cold, damp land he would need to know what sort of welcome awaited him before he undertook the long journey north.

To his delight, he had received a report back that confirmed his estate at l'Amaury was in robust health, and contained large parts of the Forest of Rambouillet, being well run and in substantial surplus by the current tenants. He resolved to reward them generously upon his reclaiming of the estates, and mentioned to Eleanor that he would be settling there after a short stay in Castres. She had merely nodded and said that before they travelled north she really would like to visit the Monastery of St Anthony at La Val Dieu, a few days ride away. She had that look in her eye and Henri pushed the obvious question to the back of his mind.

Eleanor, on Bertrand's arm, had reached him, and now stood by his side. Bertrand had uncharacteristically taken a step back and was content to let the ceremony be conducted by the Anthonine Abbot. Henri looked at Eleanor, beautiful and radiant. Managing a small blush, she gazed back at him. Her sparkling eyes met his, and his heart leapt. Henri turned as he heard the priest approaching along the chancel to begin the solemn ceremony. Through the rood screen the eyes of the priest regarded Henri for a moment before the doors of the rood swung open.

One of the few occasions the priesthood would mingle with the congregation was a wedding; usually the mass was carried out beyond the screen away from the prying ignorant eyes of the populace.

The Latin verses droned on as the priest asked, 'Who giveth this woman?'

Bertrand stepped forward and offered Eleanor's slim hand to the priest. As he did so, Bertrand's and Henri's eyes met. In that moment Henri felt as if the depths of his soul were torn open to this man. He felt—no, he *knew*, with utter certainty, that only death would part him from Eleanor, and for that matter, Bertrand.

As Henri left the Abbey with Eleanor on his arm, he saw that low grey clouds had replaced the wintry sun, and the first flakes of snow were beginning to fall. Fully expecting to be housed on his Estate, Henri had been unable attempt to obtain quarters for himself and his new bride, and it was with grateful thanks that they had accepted the offer of the Abbot's rooms for a week or so prior to their onward journey.

Bertrand had taken over an inn in the village, across the raging river Agout. One evening, soon after their wedding, the radiant couple accepted the Bishop's invitation to dine in his quarters above the inn.

Bertrand had already taken the large throne-like chair at the head of the table. Henri noticed that surprisingly the man who was, in effect, his father-in-law was wearing the black habit embroidered with the Blue Tau Crosses of an Anthonine monk. A gold chain of Office proclaimed him Grand Prior of the Order. Bertrand motioned him to be seated, but said little as the food and wine were being served. As the door closed behind the serving women, he rose and drew the heavy curtain over it. Returning to the table, he seated himself again, lowering his voice to a murmur so that Henri and Eleanor had to lean across the table to catch his words. Their three heads close together in the guttering yellow candlelight, Bertrand began to speak. 'I want to talk to you of the responsibilities that your marriage to Eleanor brings. The de Gothia Family is as ancient and distinguished as your own. We have both fought the Infidel side by side on the same battlefield many times before. Although your family has its origins amongst the Norsemen and ours stems from Visigoth Nobility we have common ancestors from the royal houses of both Aquitaine and Aragon. In fact our Coat of Arms is the same as the Aragons. Lady Eleanor holds the *de jure* title of Marquise of Gothia, because Gilbert is the progeny of my brother Wilfred's morgantic marriage, and therefore unable to inherit his father's title. Now, through this marriage, this title passes to you. At your wedding ceremony you also became a Knight of St Anthony, both these titles bind you to King James of Aragon's fight against the Infidel in Spain, so your Holy War is by no means over. From what I know of you, I am sure that you will take your responsibilities very seriously. Now, about the Templars, they have a new Grand Master, a Jacques de Molay, who is plotting and planning the return of the Crusaders to the Holy Land, but there is little enthusiasm for such a venture in France.'

Henri himself was no admirer of the Templars; he blamed them personally for the loss of the Holy Land, and as Bertrand continued he began to understand the strong undercurrents of resentment against the Templars in France. The envious and debt ridden French King, Philippe le Bel, and the overt posturing of the Templars, flaunting their wealth and their secret banking system, made it worse. Even so, the rest of Bertrand's whispers around the table that wintry night in Castres left Henri's amazed over the implications of his marriage to Eleanor.

The next morning a warm wind sprung up, and the covering of snow began to melt. As Bertrand had arranged, two beautiful fresh horses had appeared at the Inn. Eleanor, already dressed in furs for the journey ahead, was the first to vault into the saddle. With a laugh and a shout of, 'Come on, my darling Lord, race me,' she galloped off up the muddy track. With a resigned oath Henri followed, glancing back as his mount cleared the outskirts of the village.

Bertrand de Gothia, Bishop of Bordeaux, who was secretly much more, stood in the centre of the road, solemnly making the sign of the cross after the departing couple.

CHAPTER ELEVEN

It was late January 1292 and in spite of the southerly location of Castres the sky was leaden, and snow-filled flurries of wind gusted around the heavily wrapped riders.

Henri had pushed Bertrand's conversation as to his obligations to the back of his mind as he galloped off in pursuit of Eleanor. After two days of alternate furious galloping and long sensual evenings spent in small taverns, Henri was surprised to come upon a mule train, carrying the cargoes of the *Bethania* and *Bethel*, winding its steady way along tree lined tracks. He and Gilbert, who was leading the train, exchanged shouts of greetings and although Henri found it a remarkable coincidence that they were together again; he said little.

Aeons ago at the end of the last Ice Age, the mountains of the Alps and Pyrenees had discharged their swollen melt water into the basin of southern Gaul and Aragon. Drained principally by the rivers Madeleine, Aude, Sals and Rialsesse, the former seabed of the inland tropical sea had risen inexorably with the lessening of the weight of the ice, and the outpourings of glacial melt water had exploited the natural characteristics of the limestone beds.

Overlaying an older bed of shale, the pervious limestone quickly eroded through its natural faults of grykes and clints, to provide deep valleys and fast rushing rivers. Occasionally the rivers would run fast and furiously down a valley only to disappear down a sinkhole, leaving the downstream section of the valley mysteriously dry. Sometimes the river would surface further down the same valley. Wisps of steam arose from small gushing tributaries.

Wonderingly Henri dipped his hand into the water. It was at blood temperature.

'These hot springs feed my bath,' Eleanor said, as she watched his face. Her use of the word bath conjured up such a long lost memory of childhood domesticity that he shook his head sadly and then, remembering the night before's lovemaking, smiled at his lovely bride.

'Ice falling from the sky.' He indicated the dying flurries of snow. 'Bath water that comes from the ground, what other magic awaits us?'

Eleanor smiled at him before turning and galloping off with a peal of laughter, calling back to him, 'Me, me!'

The little convoy wound its way through this mysterious region of the Massif du Canigou. The result of millions of years of geological action had produced an area not unlike a giant honeycomb. At every turn monstrous cliffs and hanging valleys revealed themselves. The wooden wheels and muted conversations did little to disturb the cry of buzzards and kites as they wheeled overhead in the azure blue sky. Presently Eleanor called a halt and to Henri's puzzlement supervised the ripping of many hessian sacks into long lengths, which she had the carters wrap around the wheels of the wagons. Smaller pieces were tied to the hooves of the horses and the feet of the carters. Soon after starting off again they came to a deep, fast flowing river more than fifty yards across, its currents and eddies apparent on the surface as it flowed swiftly on.

Henri rose slightly in his stirrups, casting curious glances up and down the river. The trail had led them directly to the riverbank. To his left and right the river ran swift and deep in between walls of polished limestone. Only the track they had been travelling on penetrated the steep walls. An occasional creeper dangling in the current gave an indication of the speed of this obstacle. He half turned in the saddle, ready to halt the convoy.

'Keep onwards, Henri,' came Gilbert's urgent shout. Henri looked at him a moment longer, then urged his mount forward.

The lead wagon was about to enter the water following two of the escorting monks. The horses had shied at first, when the thick sacking had been tied round their hooves. They looked comical, almost as if wearing slippers, but once they entered the water and it rose above their fetlocks they forged onwards against the pull of the current. Below the translucent surface Henri could see the outline of huge paving blocks; the continuation of the track under water, upon which the hessian wrapped wagon wheels travelled. The blocks had been carefully fitted together, and at their edges Henri could see into the green translucent depths of the river. By now the two lead horses, obviously accustomed to the crossing, had neared the halfway mark. The reason for the wrapping of the hooves and wheels became clear; the slippery strands of waving algae on the smooth paving blocks would have afforded little grip in the strong current. Without this clever addition, the horses and carts would have been swept away downstream to the roaring plume of spray just visible as the river rounded yet another bend.

Henri's horse clambered up the gently sloping bank, and he turned to watch as the laden wagons crossed the river. He mused that if this marked the outer defence of their destination, then it had been incredibly well engineered, with more than a hint of a military mind, some considerable time ago, which did seem strange considering that he had been told that their destination was a monastery not a fortress.

Gilbert halted the convoy as the last wagons cleared the river, water cascading from them. The hessian wrappings were removed

That night the convoy dined on the plump rabbits abounding in the lush valleys. Knowing no fear of man, it was a simple matter to approach one from behind and dispatch it with a single blow. It was as though the river crossing had led them to a secret kingdom within a kingdom, and having crossed the river, Henri swore he felt the mood of the convoy lighten.

Gilbert and Eleanor, wise in the ways of this hidden world, ensured that all the bark was removed from the wood that had been gathered for the fire so as to create clear burning, almost smokeless embers on which to roast the small carcasses. All seemed at peace — except that Henri thought he had seen dark-robed figures on the rocky ramparts above the track watching them, but when he shielded his eyes against the bright sun, they had gone. Travel weariness, must have been making his eyes play tricks on him, he thought, and yet...

Eleanor woke him at dawn with a light ethereal kiss on his eyelids. Instantly he wrapped his arms around her. Alert in a second and rolling nimbly away, she grinned and rolled her eyes at the sleeping forms around them. 'Not now, my stallion!' she chuckled. 'By tonight we will have completed our journey.' She paused. 'Home.'

'Home?' Henri gave a wry smile. It was a word that had been absent from his life for many years, and certainly nothing to do with either his forgotten mouldering estate in Castres, or his ultimate destination of l'Amaury. But how could a monastery be home? He wondered. Yet again he felt himself being pulled in a direction of which he knew nothing.

The mood in the camp was light hearted that morning. For the first time many of the monks that had accompanied Gilbert with the convoy threw back their dark cowls and revelled in the bright early sun. Used as he was to dealing with fighting men under his command, Henri recognised that these Anthonines were also military men. Hard, tough-looking men, bronzed by suns far fiercer than those of Southern Europe, they were clearly anticipating with relish the moment they arrived back at their base. Henri caught the mood of the men as he rode at the head of the wagons with Gilbert. Again, he glimpsed shadowy figures on the surrounding hills, and this time there was no mistake. But Gilbert either didn't notice or abstained from commenting. Chatting easily the two men, the questioner and the questioned, rode onwards.

Gilbert gave little away to Henri's insistent probing, but did admit that the place—he spoke of it as a sanctuary—for which they were heading had been in existence for over five hundred years. Construction had been started shortly after the Battle of Poitiers in

732, and continued during the reign of Charlemagne. He did not elaborate further.

A shout from ahead alerted Henri. One of the soldiers who had accompanied them from Acre was wheeling his horse around, muttering and cursing. Henri could see a cluster of derelict buildings and hovels and, amongst them, movement. He spurred his mount forward, and two men rose from where they had been squatting. Dressed in rags and with their faces wound about with crudely wrapped bandages, they shuffled towards him. He stared, transfixed. In places the bandages had slipped to reveal horribly disfigured faces covered with open running sores. He recoiled. Eleanor's calm voice cut through to him.

'Lepers, Henri, lepers. Only the ignorant think it is transmitted by touch. These men can do you no harm.'

Her cool-voiced authority calmed him, and the soldier and the little convoy trotted past the colony of lepers. Gilbert turned and glanced at him.

'These are just some of the guardians of the Valley of God and the Monastery of St Anthony.'

Henri's heart raced. At last, an answer, a reason.

Ahead the trail curved slightly to the right, joining the bed of a small stream, no more than a bullock's cart width, before disappearing between two towering limestone buttresses. At the top of the buttresses, sentinel-like, stood two dark-robed figures, each armed only with a staff. They remained there as the convoy splashed up the narrow stream bed, its clear, warm waters barely covering the horses' hooves. Mist filled the narrow defile. For almost five hundred yards the convoy proceeded in silence, the blue sky glimpsed through the ethereal vapours, framed by the top of the polished limestone walls either side. Occasionally the shell of some long dead sea creature showed embedded in the rock. Henri turned briefly in his saddle and saw that the entire convoy was now close-bunched inside the towering walls. He frowned. A perfect ambush, he thought, his military mind still active.

The shallow waters of the steam gradually petered out, and now the horses were walking through the fine limestone dust of the dry streambed. Ahead the narrow band of blue sky began to widen. Henry felt excitement rise in him. With an exultant cry he suddenly urged his horse forward, and came thundering out of the narrow defile into open country.

He stopped just as suddenly, causing Gilbert to utter a colourful oath as he almost collided with him. The two riders paused. An incredible vista had opened in front of them.

They saw before them an enormous valley; what would have been perhaps a sinkhole or lake; a relic of the end of the last Ice Age. As the water receded it had left a deep depression some half a mile in diameter, ringed by vertical limestone cliffs. The valley was completely enclosed save for the narrow entrance to the defile from which they had just emerged. The ancient alluvial lakebed was obviously highly fertile, and stooped figures could be seen in the neat ordered fields, which were bounded by low stone walls. Carts piled high with crops made their way across the fields. Figures, dwarfed by the distance, slowly followed bullock-drawn ploughs. Below the rim of the bowl, under dangling creepers, natural caves gaped, set in the limestone cliffs. Gradually, on closer inspection, these seemed to take on a more ordered look. Crudely carved steps could be seen running up the cliffs and disappearing into the entrances many feet above the floor of the valley. Henri was able to make out lines of regular mortar joints, and the outline of windows in the walls, behind which he could see movement. The sound of distant voices floated down. The inhabitants of this extraordinary basin lived in the rock face itself!

As he watched, entranced, he saw children playing on the steps and balconies, women leaning out of windows yelling and scolding. His horse whinnied and stirred impatiently. Still Henri stared. For it was not the ordered fields, or the dwellings of the troglodytes, or the teeming abundant life he saw that transfixed him. In the centre of this secret sanctuary, dominating everything, was an incredible vision—a castle. It was a magical sight. Massive walls of mellow, dressed limestone soared to crenulated buttresses. Beyond them, reflecting the light, the conical tile roof of the inner courtyard gleamed. From the four corners pennants of the Order of St

Anthony flew bravely in the light breeze. The whole scene glittered and shone like a jewel in the pale sunlight.

A broad road, beginning at the entrance to the defile from which the rest of the convoy was still emerging, ran straight to the foot of the mighty walls, ending at a portcullis. Even as Henri watched, the distant portcullis, dwarfed like the figures in the fields, began to move slowly upwards. Now with Eleanor and Gilbert at his side he urged his mount forward down the long road that led to the bewitching castle beaming like a child on Christmas morn.

CHAPTER TWELVE

On either side of the road stretched fields, interspersed with orchards, their trees in neat orderly rows. Well-kept beehives nestled beneath them. Even though it was winter, the sky was a clear blue and all around there was a feeling of rich husbandry and contentment. As the friends drew near Henri saw, with astonishment, that the castle had been modelled on the great Castle at Jerusalem, upon whose sacred soil Henri had never set foot, but whose recapture was not only his own reason for existence, but that of all Christendom.

But this Castle did not have the hordes of colourful, teeming noisy humanity, nor the low crowded dwellings that Jerusalem had lapping at its walls. As the party drew nearer, Henri made out tiny figures patrolling the battlements; figures in glinting armour, figures with the flapping black surcoats and the emblazoned blue Tau cross of the Knights of the Order of St Anthony.

He turned in bewilderment to Gilbert, and then to Eleanor. The pair was watching him intensely, their expressions giving nothing away. Gilbert spoke at last, as if to break the spell,

'Welcome to la Val Dieu, Henri.' His voice was impassive.

'And to our future,' added Eleanor.

Her eyes seemed to sparkle suddenly. An odd little smile played briefly about her lips. For a brief moment Henri experienced a feeling made up in equal parts of anticipation and apprehension.

Entering the courtyard, after an exultant gallop along the roadway, the friends stopped in the centre of the wondrous castle. The dozen or so wagons from Narbonne followed them into the courtyard, and then veered slowly to the left, where they disappeared down some kind of curved roadway. Watching them, Henri's eyes narrowed.

'Four missing, Gilbert?'

'Not missing Henri, we sent the last four northwest to La Rochelle.' Gilbert paused, and Henri spoke impatiently.

'Go on man, why? Why have four wagons go to La Rochelle?' He saw that Gilbert didn't quite meet his eyes.

'I've sent Claude, my best sergeant, and a dozen men to escort them. They're to seek a ship at La Rochelle belonging to Prince St Clair, bound for his castle at Roslin, in Scotland for he is our Grand Prior in Scotland,' Gilbert replied.

Henri, realising that his question had not so much been answered as deflected, decided not to press the matter for the moment. But he was aware of a growing feeling of disquiet, and this mood gradually increased over the next few weeks, as Eleanor remained closeted for many hours during the day with Gilbert in the large panelled library of the inner keep, while Henri explored the estate alone. On one occasion he had knocked on the doors and without waiting for an answer had entered the room. The two were seated with an elderly Brother of the Order at the huge circular table. The monk quickly pulled his habit across his chest, but not before Henri had glimpsed the crimson breast and gold chain of office of a Cardinal

The three had been poring over a large, somehow familiar ledger bound in leather. A worn dusty satchel, last seen by Henri being carried by Gilbert from the Gate of St Anthony, Acre, lay discarded on the floor. Gilbert had risen, smiling easily, indicating that he and Eleanor were busy with affairs of their Estate. Still smiling, he had led Henri gently but firmly back through the Library doors.

Barely able to conceal his chagrin, Henri had left the inner keep and found his mount tethered in the stables. Riding furiously along the causeway he had flown through the narrow defile until he brought up at the fast flowing river. He jumped from his horse and angrily kicked at a stone, sending it hurtling into the river.

'In God's name!' he muttered to himself. 'Thrown out of the Holy Land with a King's ransom in treasure, married before I can shake a stick, and now shut out of affairs and plots of which I know nothing, as if I were a child, and what of the obligations that Bernard had discussed?'

Across the years the memory of his austere father flowed back towards him. At once his burst of temper evaporated; was replaced by cold, angry logic. He stared at the figures high above the valley, their cowls up, their dark robes flapping in the wind that blew across the Forest of Rialsesse. Setting his jaw he jumped on his mount and galloped furiously back through the defile.

This time, finding Eleanor alone in the library, he entered, slamming the door behind him. She turned, startled, from the blazing fire. A half smile froze on her lips as she saw the look upon his face.

'The roof turret, now!' he snapped.

The circular turret room at the top of the keep had a steep, conical roof. The chimneys from the great hall and the kitchens below meant that the stone inner walls seeped warmth into the narrow room. It was a place of utter privacy as the couple had discovered before. It was also soundproof, high above the bustle of the castle. Henri and Eleanor were both breathing heavily as the door closed behind them and he turned to her, his eyes cold.

'Ever since our departure from Acre,' he began, 'I have allowed myself to be guided along this gilded path by yourself and Gilbert, not questioning, but believing that in some way a future awaited me, us…And now I find myself, whilst not a prisoner, almost a hostage in this great castle, itself unknown and hidden from the world. I have been forced from the land where my Father was so brutally murdered, with no chance now of ever avenging that deed, save to languish on my estates. I have no role to play here, Eleanor except that of your husband, and it is plain that the Order to which you both belong is averse to involve me in any way.'

He had by now calmed somewhat, and was puzzled by Eleanor's silence. She merely leant against the door and observed him with a quizzical half smile. He continued.

'Before sunset tomorrow I will travel to my estate at Montfort l'Amaury in the north.'

CHAPTER THIRTEEN

Elanor looked at her husband, her face uncharacteristically betraying a fleeting series of emotions. She shook her head suddenly, as if making up her mind.

'We did not meet by chance Henri. Your great-uncle Simon was of invaluable assistance many years ago to the cause against the betrayal of Christ by the Cathar heretics. Without his help this fortification would be known to the world. History will remember Simon de Montfort for the massacres at Beziers, but believe me when I say the end justified the means. Before him, your ancestors in turn defeated the Infidel at Poitiers, a battle that my ancestors also fought at, repelling the attempted invasion by the Infidels in 732. It was, in fact, in the pursuit of the defeated followers of Mohammed, that they found La Val Dieu. So you see, Henri, our journey has been long.'

She paused a moment, looking at him with those penetrating blue eyes. Not for the first time did Henri feel he could have no secrets under her gaze.

'We still have a long, long way to go,' she concluded.

Henri's mood had become calmer. He leant against the parapet watching Eleanor without speaking, letting the warm breeze caress his face. She returned his gaze with equanimity. The silence hung between them. At last Eleanor stirred.

'Wait here.'

She turned and was gone before Henri could protest. He stared out of the roof turret. The scene around him was one of utter contentment; He felt it beginning to penetrate him. Somehow he knew that in spite of his ultimatum to Eleanor he would be part of this place for a very long time.

He heard the door open behind him and suddenly Eleanor was by his side again. Her face was flushed, and she looked at him with shining eyes. She began softly but with calm authority.

'Our battle for the Holy Land is lost for the moment, but our war with the Infidel continues for us and our future generations. Let there be no doubt, here at Val Dieu we have the means for victory, God willing.' She held out her hand to Henri. 'There is something you must see. The time has come.'

She led him back to the Library. Carefully closing and bolting the doors behind her, she walked to the table. A lamp stood there. In its pool of amber light lay a vellum map, weighed down at its four corners by heavy golden coins. Taking up one of the coins, Eleanor began.

'The centre of the map is the Castle you now stand in, and represents us, our world, our kingdom, our home. All around us are the valleys and foothills of the Massif du Carrigou, the Razes and the forest of Railesse which is our veil from prying eyes and the attentions of the world.'

'At seven or eight open points in the valleys we came through earlier are our first lines of defence. As you already know, l'Ermitage and others are our own leper colonies. Our other centres contain sufferers of St Anthony's Fire.' She seemed not to notice Henri's sudden look of horror.

'As I said earlier, leprosy is not contagious, and we know how to control St Anthony's Fire.' She paused, glancing at him. Henri nodded, remembering Cyprus.

'The only villages in the vicinity are the two Rennes, Rennes Le Bains and Rennes Le Chateau. These are now mere fractions of their ancient size, as much of the original Visigoth settlements were demolished to provide the means to build Val Dieu. In both those villages we have our own eyes and ears.'

Henri waited for her to elaborate on this. Instead she went on, 'Inwards from the colonies we patrol the heights of the valleys ourselves, and as you've seen, the final approach is well concealed.

We have been here for over five hundred years and no one knows about us who should not.'

The "We" seemed to hang in the air between them. There had been a sense of implacability — a kind of baleful malignance in her words that had sent a chill through Henri. For a moment the expression of agonized shock on the face of Rodger de Flor as Eleanor's steel entered his brain flashed before him. In what seemed an oddly conciliatory gesture Eleanor, took his hand and kissed him lightly.

'Please my Lord, keep your questions until later, now we go to the vaults.'

Leaving the inner keep, they entered the main courtyard inside the massive portcullis through which they galloped on that first day. To the left of this a road curved into what Henri saw was the entrance to a passageway, after which it descended steeply. Pausing only to provide themselves with torches, the pair began the journey that would lead them deep into the bowels of the castle.

The surface of rough-hewn cobbles had been worn in two parallel grooves by the passage of many wheels over the centuries. Overhead the walls curved into a smooth arch, and Henri marvelled at the skill of the ancient stonemasons. Not a feather's thickness could penetrate the joints of the stone blocks. Down, down they went bearing constantly to the right. It seemed to Henri that they had turned back on themselves three times, and still the flickering light revealed the passageway stretching downwards. A fresh, gentle breeze coming from somewhere moved gently around them, making the light from the torches dance and sway. Still they descended — until at last they arrived at two immense iron-studded wooden doors.

Eleanor gave Henri a reassuring glance, and then knocked on it seven times. A small section of one of the doors slid open, and a single eye regarded them. Then the sound of heavy bolts being drawn back echoed along the passage. Before the door was fully open, Eleanor slipped through, drawing Henri with her. Taking both torches, she extinguished them in a vat of water standing by.

Henri froze. They had stepped into dazzling sunshine. The light poured down past hanging creepers and lianas. They were in a huge roofless chamber, at whose furthest extremity Henri could barely discern a number of robed figures moving quickly, apparently engaged in some kind of labour. To one side a long column of untended carts such as he had escorted to this place stretched away from him. At the head of the column, where the carts were being unloaded, furnaces glowed. Clouds of smoke and steam coiled skywards, dissipating slowly.

Henri gazed in wonder at this mighty roofless cathedral; its natural rock walls sloping inwards to the patch of iridescent blue hundreds of feet above his head. The vertical rock walls would have ended in a jagged gash framing the sky but for the softening effect of the flora hanging into this secret world.

Letting go of Eleanor's hand, Henri walked slowly down the line of waiting carts, his fingers lightly brushing their coarse bodywork. Different styles of construction, some ornate and carved, some plain workaday farm carts, spoke of their origins from different countries, different regions. The carts he had seen being loaded at Narbonne with the cargoes of the *Bethel* and the *Bethania* had now been joined by many others, all crowding into this enormous cavern. The single factor linking all the wagons—he calculated that there must be about eighty of them—was that, evidenced by their sagging bodywork, they each carried a very heavy load.

He turned as Eleanor's light footsteps sounded behind him. Wordlessly she took his hand and led him farther along the chamber to the roaring furnaces. There were three of them, stood against the sloping rock wall. Henri watched as one by one the wagons, having been emptied of their precious cargo, were broken up and pushed into the furnace to feed the hungry flames. The heat was intense. Moving aside a little to try and escape it, Henri glimpsed what, to his overwrought imagination, seemed to be a vision of Hell.

To each furnace was attached a large bellows made of wood and covered with animal hide. These were connected by a crude, yet complicated arrangement of rods and wheels. The whole system was kept in motion by the pumping feet of three small dark creatures wearing heavy iron collars around their necks, which were attached to the wall behind them. Moving between the three bellows, carrying an ox hide whip, strode a huge Nubian—a slave-master.

In the flickering light his black skin shone with sweat. His rippling muscles bulged as with liberal use of the whip he urged the three slaves to greater efforts on their tread mills.

A pair of sweating, leather clad foundry men was ladling molten metal in a golden stream into moulds of sand. The fiery liquid hissed and spluttered, sending showers of sparks into the air.

Eleanor touched Henri's arm. 'Come now,' she mouthed. He followed her to a stone wall, twice the height of a man. A door had been let into it. It opened at Eleanor's touch. Henri followed her through it. At once the noise and heat were cut off as she closed the door behind them.

They were in a place of pure magic. To the faint sound of rushing, tumbling water the walls danced and spun with a myriad of shifting light patterns. All was brightness, radiance and dazzling luminosity.

At a table sat four men wearing the dark habit and blue Tau cross of the Anthonines. Henri saw that they were engaged in carefully dismantling a great mound of gold and silver relics, chalices, swords, chains of office, all richly encrusted with jewels. It was these that were giving off the brilliant dancing colours that raced across the grey stonewall.

Henri was accustomed to a fairly ostentatious show of wealth. But here, jumbled and piled like so much flotsam and jetsam, lay much, much more than even a king's ransom—the spoils of war from two hundred years of crusading against the Infidel.

Behind each of the Brothers there stood a large reed basket. As the treasure was dismantled, using crude picks, hammers and chisels, the golden metal mounts were put into the basket. As these were filled, they were moved by other robed figures to the arched door leading to the furnace room. The precious stones extracted by the delicate picks were placed in a leather container. Henri saw that it was three quarters full of gemstones, from small pea-sized pearls to rubies, emeralds, sapphires, and diamonds, many as large as a bird's egg. 'There's more,' Eleanor whispered in his ear, disturbing his reverie.

He glanced at her, and then about him. He saw that there were passages leading off the main chamber like the spokes of a wheel. Sturdy wooden racks could be seen at the entrances to these passages. Each rack was made up of ten shelves on which were stacked row on row of yellow-gold ingots. The racks, burdened with their gleaming cargo, stretched into the passageways until they were lost in darkness.

Henri turned to look at Eleanor. Standing quietly there, she seemed both fragile and indomitable, a paradox set against a backdrop of incredible industry. Smiling slightly, her face pale in the glancing light, she took his hand again, leading him this time towards where the sound of running water was coming from; to where, in the farthest reaches of the chamber, a broad, fast-flowing river ran.

Here there was little light. The river, black and swift and somehow ominous, both appeared and disappeared into the rock itself. A small rope bridge precariously spanned the rushing, swirling torrent. Eleanor confidently placed her foot on the bridge, beckoning him to follow. In a moment, though it seemed longer to Henri, they found themselves on a wide rock shelf, with only the rushing depths separating them from the rest of the cavern.

Yet another door was set into the rock. This opened onto a narrow stone staircase. A thick rope was attached to the walls with rusty iron stanchions. There were no torches here to light the way. Leaving the sound of the rushing waters behind them they began to climb into darkness using the rope as a guide.

The stairs seemed to go on forever. After a while Henri's calf muscles began to ache, his heart to pound. About to protest, he heard Eleanor ahead of him fumble with something that sounded metallic, and immediately the narrow staircase was flooded with radiance. They stepped into a room of light; a circular room panelled on the floor and walls in the palest of oak. The source of the amazing brilliance came from the many wide windows let into the walls of the room; windows that had nothing in common with the more usual arrow-slits.

Wonderingly Henri walked across this silent glowing room and touched the translucent material. Slight imperfections in the surface made the reflection of the countryside beyond shimmer and dance. Outside the banners streaming from the turrets snapped and cracked in the stiff breeze, but the room was a haven of light, air and tranquillity.

Since he was little more than a child Henri had heard talk of this wonderful new material called 'glass', brought back from the Wars by Flemish soldiers. It was so expensive, it was said, that only the very rich, the nobles, the merchants grown fat on prosperity, could afford it. His fingers stroked it gently. He turned to see that Eleanor was standing at the opposite side of the room. While he had been musing she had slipped off her voluminous cloak. And then he saw what was behind her upon an altar and gasped.

Upon the altar standing over six feet high stood a huge golden seven branched candelabrum.

'As you know Henri, my ancestors were Visigoth nobility, and when they sacked Rome in 410 they captured this sacred Menorah which the Romans had looted from the Temple of Solomon in Jerusalem and brought it here to Rhedae their capital. In 700 it was returned to the Jews here in Narbonne where their royal family resided. Just before Narbonne fell to the Infidel in 720 this Menorah and other of their holy treasures was taken by them and hidden at the monastery of Guilhem le Desert, and when our Sanctuary was ready in 895 it was brought here. From that point on this place has been the Treasure House of our Holy Order Treasures that we guard on behalf of our Holy Church and use on its behalf to fight its Holy War.'

She stood there in a simple white satin sheath, which fell sheer to her ankles. Her slim waist was circled by a broad leather belt, from which hung a sword, a thing of ancient jewelled beauty that glittered, throwing back the light. 'This is Joyeuse The Sword of

Charlemagne and this...' In her right hand she held a golden chalice, tall and thin-stemmed; it flared almost sensuously into a bowl flanked by two graceful handles.

Without asking—hardly daring to breath—Henri knew what that chalice was.

One of the reasons for the bloody crusading quests into the Holy Land, started by Urban II in 1095, and urged on with fanatical zeal by subsequent Popes, was the race to find the most sacred vessel of Christendom—The Chalice of the Eucharist—the cup from which Jesus had drunk at the last supper, and which was said to hold a drop of His Holy blood. It was thought that possession of this sacred cup not only gave the alluring promise of eternal life, but also of temporal Power greater than anyone had ever known.

When Joseph of Aramethia was cast into prison following the death of Jesus, Christ himself had miraculously appeared to him and had given him this vessel. By it he was sustained in his solitary confinement, which lasted for two years until he was freed by the Emperor Vespasian. According to legend, Joseph, or his colleague, Lissan, had taken the Grail to Glastonbury in England. Following Joseph's death the Grail had mysteriously disappeared, to the anguish of the Christian world.

All this went through Henri's mind as, unable to speak, unable to move, he watched Eleanor pour the flagon's contents into the gleaming bowl.

She offered it to him. Trance like, he took a deep draught of the aromatic ruby wine, then watched as she did the same. She then unbuckled the Sword and handed it to him. 'This now belongs to you my Prince, and in turn it shall belong to our descendants.' Then she turned and walked towards the huge four-poster bed that stood under one of the windows.

Sunlight streamed through her fine satin garment, which she now let slip from her onto the flag-stoned floor. Holding his gaze, she stretched out on the bed, cat like, languid, smiling. He moved towards her, towards the promise in her smile, knowing that somehow a point of no return had been passed; he had finally and irrevocably been accepted not only by his beloved, but also by the power she represented. She was preparing to lead him, with her secret, mystic power, into something shadowy-deep and profoundly mysterious; something as yet unnamed, but that would shape his life and the Fate of his family forevermore. There were sudden tears in his eyes, but his heart soared as he walked towards her.

The sun casting its fiery rays through the windows woke them. They dressed without speaking, but sending each other faint, smiling glances. Something had changed between them—now there was no looking back.

Finally able to take in the details of the room, Henri saw that there was another door opposite the one they had entered—how long ago that seemed now! A spirit of joyous, almost childlike mischief made him turn the handle and peer round the edge. The door opened onto a balcony running round the walls of a great hall. He frowned, not recognising this part of the castle.

From behind him Eleanor said softly, 'We are not inside the castle now, my lover. We are in the Observetoire La Pique.' Smiling at him in her enigmatic way she led Henri along the balcony. In the hall below them, two mighty chandeliers hung over a table spread magnificently for four people. For the second time that day, used, as he was, to displays of wealth, Henri marvelled at the richness and opulence of the surroundings, at last realising that all this wealth was theirs to dispose of as they wished. His own small estates now seemed irrelevant. He was now part of something much larger than being yet another feudal baron.

Eleanor opened a small door that led onto the roof of what Henri now realised was the monastery. The stiff breeze had freshened, become almost fierce, causing the streaming banners to flap noisily.

At one end of the roof stood the figure of a man in a billowing robe, his back to them. He turned as they approached. His eyes were cold and grey, his face set. He extended a large hand. 'Henri, its good to see you again.' His expression gave nothing away. Henri wordlessly returned the handshake. Eleanor said, 'Hello, Uncle Bertrand,' and embraced him affectionately.

'But of course,' Henri thought, 'of course.'

Now he knew his place. Now he knew that because of these two he had become a part of something extraordinary

But a part of—what?

Bertrand put his arm around Henri's shoulders, and with Eleanor on his other arm began slowly to pace with them the length of the roof.

'You must know,' he said, his head turning slightly in Henri's direction so that there was no doubt about to whom he was speaking, 'You must know that following the recent death of His Holiness, Pope Nicholas IV, the Council of Cardinals...' His voice took on a faint edge, '...have done again that which they do best, they have elected a frail elderly hermit, Pope Celestine V, because they could not agree on anybody else, and as he is approaching eighty years of age it gives us a little time to prepare the ground for our next candidate.'

Henri glanced quickly at Eleanor. For a bishop to be discussing the College of Cardinals' choice of the next Vicar of Christ betrayed an extraordinary level of confidence, he thought.

'We shall choose a Pope who will stand up to the intrigues and plotting of Philippe le Bel,' Bertrand said. 'The King of France makes new demands daily, taxing the Church in order to fatten his own purse, and to fund his war with England. I tell you, Henri that the King of France is heavily in debt to the Knights Templar, and is even now looking for ways to abrogate that debt.'

Henri frowned. 'And this election of a weak, eighty year old Pope will achieve what exactly?'

Bertrand acknowledged this question, but did not reply directly. Instead he led them from the roof down a narrow staircase to the peace and warm tranquillity of the Great Hall.

The figure now seated at the magnificently set table rose as they approached. Bertrand made the introductions. 'May I present my niece, the Lady Eleanor, and her husband, Lord Henri de Montfort l'Amaury. Eleanor—Henri—this is Cardinal Gaetani.'

Having completed the introductions he seated himself, motioning the others to do the same, and clapped his hands sharply. Soft-footed Brothers of the Order appeared carrying steaming dishes.

The meal was superb. During it nothing of importance was discussed. When the last dishes were cleared away, the dying fire was replenished with logs and the serving Brothers retired, closing the door with respectful bows. For a while there was silence. Then Cardinal Gaetani rose and stood before the fire nursing a large goblet.

'The war in the East is over, as you know, Henri,' he said. 'We cannot fight a thousand miles from home from a fractured Europe with indifferent support. The Saracens are united in purpose and fear no man, indeed their death in battle is taught as an immediate entry to paradise itself.' His eyes sought and held Henri's.

This man knows of my Hashashin past Henri mused as he listened.

Gaetani continued, 'You have seen today our preparations for the continuance of that war, which our learned Urban II began two hundred years ago in Clermont. France and other nations emptied themselves of Knights and warriors to go Eastwards, but on our own borders in Al-Andalus, the Infidel have been in occupation since 711, and have changed the beliefs and social structures in that country so as to be unrecognisable to Christian men. Whilst the Holy See watches and wrings its hands at our failure in the Holy Land, the Knights of St Anthony, shielded from the world by their brothers in the Order of St Anthony, have been fighting the Infidel from here for over five-hundred years.'

Henri's thoughts went swiftly to Gilbert's comments as they were approaching the castle for the first time.

'Groups of Knights,' continued Gaetani, 'brought by Giullaume de Gellone, Compte de Razes, from their home in Ethiopia, assisted Charlemagne in 778 as he entered Iberia with the Neustrian Army to receive the homage of Solomon ibn-al-Arabi at Zaragoza, and it was their skill that prevented the massacre at Roncevaux Pass turning into a rout. I believe you and Gilbert attempted to capture the Uthman Koran at Acre, an attempt also made when the Caliph of Baghdad, Harun-al-Rashid was lured into contact with a unit of Knights in 801. That particular manuscript contains a message that we have fought to obtain for over five hundred years. So you see, Henri, our fight is long, and may grow longer, but God is on *our* side.'

His voice cracking with passion and fanatical conviction, he paused to take a long draught from his goblet.

'We now use our resources to help the Kings of Aragon and Navarre in their battles against the Caliph of Iberia. The Islamic hordes do not rule easily, and now they have declared war on the Jews and the Visigoths, and we must press this advantage.' He suddenly threw up his hands.

'But I have not come here merely to ask the help of a courageous knight for an adventure in foreign lands.' He smiled. 'We will win in Al-Andalus not only because it is our home, but the basis of this,' he indicated the large, silent hall, 'the home of the Anthonine Order, and its battle for the Holy Land. A battle which may take us into unknown waters, for I fear in future we may not rely merely on brave men in armour, but on our cunning and our great wealth, to bring about our return to Jerusalem, and in time, God willing, to bring the light of Christianity to those afflicted by the laws and customs of Islam.'

Henri waited respectfully for the Cardinal to finish before he spoke. 'Sire, with respect, how can you base your future on those assumptions if the Holy Father decides to pursue a different policy, and not involve your organisation? You plan for hundreds of years in the future, yet all is at the mercy of the decision of the incumbent Pope.'

Cardinal Gaetani regarded Henri with cold eyes 'Then we shall be requiring a new, strong-minded Pope, Henri'

The fire had not burned down all that much, but Henri felt a shiver run through him, and he suddenly realised that with its great wealth the Order of St Anthony was also in control of the Vatican itself. And this was its great secret, now his secret.

CHAPTER FOURTEEN

Henri's forays on behalf of the King of Aragon grew less as the Moors were pushed further and further south, and it came as something of a surprise when one day he idly calculated that he had not left the Castle for over a year.

While he had occasionally fretted about the lack of action, his life had become filled with the day-to-day concerns generated by maintaining the large estates, supervising the work being undertaken in the secret cavern, and his growing delight at fatherhood, now that his son, whom he named Raymond after his beloved grandfather, had been born.

If he felt that he had been somehow been excluded from Eleanor's plans so far, it was as nothing to the exclusion he had experienced at his son's birth.

Eleanor's body had swollen enormously, and at times Henri harboured the thought that their child would cause her to burst like a ripe plum. Two older women from the estates attended Eleanor as the first pains arrived. Gently but firmly they shooed Henri from the apartments, his leaving and his acceptance of their authority as much a surprise to him as to the two women.

He paced the battlements watching, but unseeing, for half a day until Eleanor's screams drove him to their bedroom door. As he reached for the door handle, the lusty cry of a newborn baby slowed his panic-stricken rush, and he entered the apartment in time to see an exhausted Eleanor cradling in her arms a well-wrapped noisy bundle, as the local women made their excuses and left.

As the door closed behind the two midwives, Eleanor slumped back in the bed, her face weary, and her eyes watchful. Henri carefully took the tiny bundle in his arms. His eyes met Eleanor's, and she nodded.

'A boy Henri, it's a boy, and just the beginning of a dynasty that will sweep the Infidel from the face of the earth.'

Henri nodded, understanding.

When he suggested to Eleanor that they call the boy Raymond, she had laughed and said

'Truly Henri you prophecy well, with all the wealth that he will have at his disposal he surely could become *Le Roi de Monde,* King of the World'

✠✠✠

Bertrand who had recently been elevated to the position of Archbishop of Bordeaux had arrived one spring morning to announce his new title to his family and to talk about the latest political machinations that he was involved with. Henri listened with interest to his accounts of the public rows between a rapacious King Philippe of France, and Pope Boniface VIII. The King's refusal to return the wealth of the Holy Mother Church to Rome that he had misappropriated, was becoming ever more adamant.

Boniface VIII had used the approaching turn of the century to call all pilgrims to Rome with their offerings. As the last years of the old century drew to a close, almost two million pilgrims filled the ancient city. Two priests reportedly stood all day and night behind the beautiful altar of St Paul using rakes and shovels to drag away the steady stream of gold and silver offered by the faithful in exchange for remission of their sins. Bertrand wryly remarked on one visit that Boniface had interpreted literally the words from his Papal investiture; 'Take the tiara, and know that thou art the father of princes and kings, the ruler of the world, the Vicar on earth of our Saviour, Jesus Christ.'

Emboldened by his newfound wealth, Boniface had determined to bring to a head the problem of Philippe IV of France, who by now had resorted to confiscating Church lands and property in lieu of unpaid taxes. To make matters worse, Boniface's sworn enemies at the Papal palace, members of the Colonna family who had railed against his investiture, had been given sanctuary by Philippe IV. In fury, Boniface summoned the Council of Cardinals in Rome, but Philippe's strength lay in his total control of the French clergy, and via their weekly sermons he rallied the French people around him against what he believed was a vicious and greedy Pope.

Philippe forbade any French prelate to attend the Council, called, he said, to denigrate the Throne of France. Disobedience would be repaid by the total confiscation of the entire Papal French property.

Yet another expedition into Castile on behalf of the King of Aragon provided Henri with much needed intelligence as he travelled, as a monk of the Order, over the Pyrenees. The content and general tendency of many of the sermons he heard preached by local priests provided him with irrefutable evidence of Philippe's meddling in the Church's affairs. He felt at times that the whole country was seething with indignation at the politicised antics of the Holy Father.

Henri had fought with many men, had killed many more, and had spent the majority of his life at war for his One True God. If he was anything at all he was an utterly loyal servant of God's representative on earth, and there were occasions when it took all his self-discipline not to reach for his sword.

One day, on returning to the castle after such a foray, he was pleased to see the personal guards of Bertrand de Gothia practising the new two-handed axe-play in the courtyard. Eagerly he sought out Bertrand, whom he had come to regard almost as a father-in-law. He found him in the library in deep and quiet discussion with Eleanor. They were sat by the fire with their heads almost touching, the murmur of their conversation lost against the crackle of the logs.

The two drew apart at Henri's entrance. Not for the first time did he feel himself in the role of a junior partner. Throwing off his frustration, he made to speak to Bertrand. Bertrand shook his head, and rose, pointing to his mouth and ears, indicating they should go onto the roof, the place of all their confidential discussions. Once there he paced between Henri and Eleanor, saying little whilst Henri told him what was troubling him.

'Philippe le Bel is bound to grant me an audience if only from curiosity,' Henri had concluded.

'Provided you keep your name from Guillaume de Nogaret,' cautioned Eleanor.
'He claims that family were burned as Cathars by Simon de Montfort and he still hates the Montfort name, he has the Kings trust and is a dangerous man'

'The question,' interrupted Bertrand, 'is this. Will Philippe's desire to abrogate his debts to the Templars cause him to be less cunning when dealing with Abbot Henri of the Order of St Anthony, supposing that he is under the impression that the Abbot can assist him in his goal?'

Henri glanced quickly at Bertrand. An Archbishop, maybe, he thought, but a clever, scheming one.

Eleanor added, 'Henri could intimate to Philippe that only through the offices of Bertrand de Gothia, Archbishop of Bordeaux and the Order of St Anthony, may it prove possible to achieve the downfall of the Templars, and the abrogation of his debts.'

Henri frowned at her. She was regarding him with a strange intense look, as if trying to compel him to follow Bertrand's lead. Bertrand spoke softly.

'Just supposing the Pope was to assist Philippe—in secret, of course—to acquire the holdings of the Knights Templar—'

Henri's face was furious, his fists clenched. 'The Knights are pledged to the Pope, My Lord! They have fought and died for him and his office. That would be treachery of the basest kind indeed.'

Bertrand raised his hand and his cold eyes bored into Henri's.

'But what if the holdings were empty? What if the majority of the Knights simply disappeared? A pyrrhic victory, perhaps?'

Leaving Henri staring after him, he turned and walked with Eleanor to the far corner of the roof. Henri stood for a long time at the battlements staring over the green and pleasant fields surrounding him. His mind raced and seethed with bewilderment and indignation. He stared balefully at the couple at the end of the roof. Their heads came together briefly. Then Bertrand turned and descended the steps to the library. Eleanor regarded Henri coolly as he approached, his face flushed with anger.

'In God's name Eleanor, you seem to have woven a spell far too strong! At every step, events that I have marvelled at turn out to be the result of long-laid plans and plots conceived even before I was born. I am defeated in the Holy Land, only to be brought here, to this secret place of fantastic wealth and then to find that I am a pawn in a game of which I know little. And now, unless I am very much mistaken, I am being asked to commit treachery against the Most Holy Order of the Temple.' Henri paused, calming himself a little as he took Eleanor in his arms. 'Knights I admit I have no love for, but who, nevertheless, have given their lives in the cause of God's Vicar on Earth. Eleanor, this man, your uncle, Archbishop, whoever, is asking me to betray men whom I have fought alongside all of my life!'

Henri pulled angrily away from Eleanor and went stamping down the stairs to the library. He burst in to find Bertrand by the fire regarding him with equanimity. The door closed behind Henri as Eleanor joined them.

'Boniface would never even speak to Philippe IV, let alone negotiate secretly,' began Henri forcefully, thinking as he said it that it was stating the obvious.

'I concur, but perhaps Philippe may be unaware he is not negotiating with the Pope,' Bertrand shot back.

Henri acknowledged the reply with a furious shake of his head. 'You still haven't answered my point,' he said forcefully.

Bertrand regarded Henri for a moment, his eyes flicking between him and Eleanor. 'A Archbishop of Bordeaux, may I remind you; and under English fealty what is more, would not offend Philippe so deeply.' Bertrand said softly, his eyes dark and direct.

Henri laughed sarcastically. 'You have my utmost respect, sir, but the King of France is not likely to confuse a Chaplain to Boniface VIII with the Papal office itself.'

Bertrand replied coldly, 'So long as I remain merely the Chaplain, I agree.'

A long silence followed this, each alone with his thoughts.

Eleanor interjected quietly. 'The English connection is a good point indeed. Philippe's war with the aggressive Edward of England is a huge drain on his resources. I am told that even now he seeks an alliance to marry his sister to Edward and his daughter to Edward's son. That union may well prove not to be as fruitful as Philippe hopes. My sources tell me the Prince of Wales prefers the flesh of men.' She smiled wryly.

'But with England placated,' mused Henri, 'at least, Philippe could turn his attention elsewhere.'

✠✠✠

Henri knelt before the Vicar of Christ on Earth at the High Altar of St Peters. It had been a considerable undertaking to gather together the band of the Brothers of St Anthony and journey to Rome. Their slow passage through the villages they passed on their journey had been greeted with a mixture of fear and loathing. Surreptitious visits days in advance of the tiny band of monks had ensured that a selected village had an outbreak of St Anthony's Fire just as, God be praised, the Brothers appeared. Usually one or two would have died in agony, their limbs blackening as their terror stricken eyes watched their own bodies putrefy. It had never occurred to the suffering villagers to connect the catastrophe that had devastated their population with the visits a day or two earlier of two merchants selling rye grain and flour.

The Monks had come to Rome to have the Order of St Anthony ordained under the rule of St Austin by Boniface VIII; a method, as Bertrand explained, of distancing themselves from the Hospitaller and especially the Templar Orders. Accordingly, in the late summer of 1297, the Order was finally ordained as Canons regular, giving them the established monastic way of living that would protect their dark secrets even more.

Henri, now officially the Abbot of the Order, had knelt before Pope Boniface VIII to receive his Papal blessing. Raising his eyes to the cross on the altar of St Peter, he caught sight of Archbishop Bertrand de Gothia, in his role as chaplain, standing to the left of the Pope. Flicking his eyes back to Boniface he felt immediately that the power of the most Holy Office on Earth had already shifted. More importantly, he felt utterly at one with his new feeling, an innate sense of inescapable destiny. As he knelt in silence, he remembered painfully the peaceful quietness of the church at Tyre moments before his father's brutal assassination. He felt as though his father had laid his hand gently upon him.

After the simple ceremony the private chapel had emptied of the curia and scribes, and Boniface once more placed his hand on Henri's bare head, looking down at the couple in front of him.

'May the blessing of God the Father be upon you, Abbot Henri and to you, Abbess Eleanor.'.

He raised his eyes and his voice thundered suddenly.

'Be it God's Holy will that the forces of evil that live within the Infidel unbelievers are finally banished from this earth.'

CHAPTER FIFTEEN

Boniface also known as the "Chequered Eagle" had continued his public war with Philippe IV, and had raised the stakes considerably by his bull: *Unam Sanctami*; the strongest claim of Papal supremacy ever issued.

'It is a condition of salvation,' he had thundered at the King of France, 'that all human beings should be subject to the Pontiff of Rome.'

In return, Philippe's loyal servant and lawyer, Guillaume de Nogaret, had prepared a legal assault on the Pope, affirming that the Church had been, in God's eyes, married to Celestine V, and that therefore Boniface, while Celestine still lived, had committed the sin of adultery by stealing away the bride of God.

De Nogaret then produced a list of twenty-nine charges against the Pope, including stealing Church property, heresy and the murder of Celestine V. Henri knew that the people of France, through Philippe's control of the Priesthood, believed these charges. It came as a shock, however, that the French Templars under Hugh de Peraud sided with the French king against their spiritual leader. Bertrand had confided in Henri that Hugh de Peraud, against all Templar Law, had become the godfather to King Philippe IV's son, in addition to lending considerable amounts of money to the French king from the Order's coffers.

Bertrand had walked with Henri from St Peters, after the Ordination of the Order, through the crowded streets of Rome, the noise and bustle providing the perfect cover for their conversation. As always, he came straight to the point.

'You should go back to Paris, Henri. Now would be an opportune moment to talk to the French King Philippe. Your wife's reading of the situation is correct. De Nogaret may indeed pose a threat, but my spies tell me he has left the French court, bound for Agagni.'

'Agagni?'

'He seeks an audience with Boniface following the announcement that the entire French Kingdom was to be excommunicated.' Bertrand paused as Henri raised his eyebrows. 'I have a suspicion the audience may not be entirely peaceful, as fifteen hundred of King Philippe's soldiers are accompanying him.'

'Are you not normally at his side?' asked Henri.

'I am Chaplain only to the Office of The Holy Father, my dear son,' Bertrand smoothly replied.

✠✠✠

Henri and the members of the Order had not dallied long in Paris, and were soon returned to their mountain sanctuary. Henri, leapt from his horse, weary with weeks of travelling, but invigorated by the prospect of being with Eleanor again. He found her in the large airy room beneath the turret roof of the castle. The bed had been removed, and now the room had become a repository of the Order's records. Over the years, every golden plate, every bezant and precious stone, had been painstakingly recorded in the red leather-bound volumes, and The Order of St Anthony was now the wealthiest institution in the World. The light, streaming through the Flemish glass, bleached the corners and edges of these rows of volumes, but every time one was removed from its shelf Henri saw in his mind's eye Gilbert descending the stone steps of the Gate of St Anthony all those years ago in Acre. Henri's strong arms encircled his wife and her swollen stomach, and he nuzzled her affectionately.

'A girl this time, I know it for sure,' he murmured.

Eleanor regarded him, eyes shining. 'Of course it is, my dear, of course,' she smiled and rested her head against his shoulder.

A clatter of hooves came from the courtyard below. Eleanor peered down through the distortions of the glass. 'Uncle!' she said, her smile widening. 'Uncle Bertrand at last. I haven't' seen him for over two years!'

Henri and Eleanor had began to be somewhat concerned when Bertrand's visits dropped off dramatically, but he had sent word that he had been at the Court of Philippe IV for a considerable time. Henri had nodded silently when he heard this.

His own sojourn there had not been in vain. Indeed Eleanor had greeted his return with considerable relief, elated to find that Henri had used the ratification of the Order to conduct negotiations with Philippe IV as Abbot Henri of the Monastery La Val Dieu.

Later that day a messenger arrived shaky and nervous. He eventually summoned the courage to speak. 'In the name of the Father, Son and Holy Ghost it is my sad duty to inform you, the people of this Holy Place, that I bring news of a dark and tragic nature.'

He paused, looking around as if seeking the courage to continue. His pale face bore a sheen of perspiration. He stood for several moments, his mouth opening, but with no sound issuing. Presently he took a deep breath and continued, 'Our Most Holy Father, Pope Boniface VIII, has died following an assault on the Papal Palace at Agagni.'

Henri leant to Eleanor and whispered, 'Agagni, that's where Philippe sent de Nogaret. Somehow he is involved in this.'

'Further, there has come a proclamation declaring Niccolo Bocassini as the next Holy Father. He has taken the name Benedict XI.'

✠✠✠

Five months after the inauguration of Benedict XI, Bertrand, who had spent several months at the castle, only occasionally disappearing for a few days, bade Henri saddle up. The pair had ridden out of the castle, and in silence traversed the causeway between a sea of early spring crops. Pausing at the narrow entrance to the defile they turned and looked back, at the castle's walls. To Henri, they had taken on an almost dreamlike quality.

The unaccompanied ride was a sufficiently rare event to have put Henri on his guard. Ruefully he remarked to Bertrand, 'Is it always the case that you need to tell me your darkest plots surrounded by nature?' Bertrand roared with laughter as he regarded Henri's expression. The horses fidgeted anticipating a good morning's exercise ahead. The movement snapped Bertrand into action and wheeling, he urged his mount down the narrow passage. The defile became wet as the path returned to the riverbed, and Bertrand's horse threw up a swirling mist of water droplets into which Henri followed.

Bertrand was a fast and confident rider, and as the trail widened into one of the valleys of the Razes, he abruptly turned onto a path heading diagonally up the side of the valley. Cresting the top of the ridge, horses and men breathless with effort, they paused to look back. As far as the distant Pyrenees, their snow-clad peaks evident even at this distance, the rolling, undulating hills and the forest clad slopes of the forest of Railesse stretched. All around them was a huge spreading canopy of green. Of their secret kingdom there was no sign.

'When man achieves the abilities of the birds,' Bertrand said eyeing the circling buzzards above, 'then we shall have to think again. Until that day I should say our secret is safe.' He smiled at Henri, but his eyes were cool and watchful. 'You are a soldier, Henri. Tell me, what is the quality you would look for most in selecting men for your troop?'

Henri paused a moment before replying carefully, 'Courage, fitness, a strong sense of purpose, and above all, an ability to follow orders.'

Bertrand nodded his eyes on the distant horizon. 'You've been here over twelve years, Henri. You have two fine children, Raymond, and, I believe, the latest addition, Maria.'

'In honour of my mother who was killed by the Infidel.'

Bertrand nodded briefly. 'Twelve years of building our sanctuary.'

Henri noted his own inclusion into the partnership.

Bertrand continued, 'So that we may continue the fight against the Islamic hordes.'

'A new crusade?' Henri interjected, his pulse quickening.

Bertrand glanced at quickly at him. 'A crusade. Yes, my dear son, but not in the way you think. We have spoken before of the need to change the fight. We must no longer think in purely military terms, or indeed…even winning the battle within our own short lives. Like the Infidel, we may have to sacrifice ourselves, but in our case it will be to bring about that which God wishes us to do. Could you do that, Henri?'

Henri nodded without hesitation.

'We may,' Bertrand said softly, 'have to betray others. Some strangers to us, yes—but also those closer to us.'

Again Henri nodded. He had reflected earlier on his time with the Hashishin, the fanatical band of Islamic fighters that Bertrand kept alluding to in his conversations with Henri. He felt now, more than anything that a task was soon to be set for him that would change his life forever.

Nothing more was said as the pair rode through the valleys, enjoying the early spring sun. Much later, as the sun lengthened the shadows, they re-entered the narrow defile, and paused again at its opening into the fertile bowl of the Sanctuary.

'I need you to go to Perugia, Henri,' said Bertrand suddenly. 'It is the home town of Benedict XI.' Bertrand gripped Henri's arm. 'I need you to practice what you learnt in the mountains above Damascus near Baalbek. See to it, Henri. We enter the next stage of our plan soon.'

He whirled his horse, and galloped furiously down the straight road to the castle.

That evening Henri saddled up and clattered back out of the castle gates, with Bertrand's word's ringing in his ears.

'Do not fail me, Henri. I shall be in Paris with Gilbert.'

If he noticed Eleanor's tearful goodbye to her brother, he did not say.

✠✠✠

Henri was accepted quickly into the Court of Benedict XI, and the Order had sufficient importance in the life of Boniface, his predecessor, to gain him a personal Papal audience. Benedict and his court of curia, selected now from both the Orsini and Colonna families of Italy, showed polite if scant interest in one Abbot Henri as he discussed the monastic rule of the Order of St Anthony in the context of the new Papal reign.

The Court at Perugia was not the largest or the most opulent of Papal residences, but Henri's sparsely furnished cell below the Pope's apartments became his home for a few months. As an Abbot of the Order of St Anthony he attracted little attention compared to the scarlet clad Cardinals that swept in and out of Benedict's court. The Pope's great age and the identity of his likely successor formed a major part of the conversations in and around the Papal Palace. Henri was not altogether surprised to discover that Archbishop Bertrand de Gothia had been retained as private chaplain to the Pope following the previous incumbent's unfortunate demise.

Henri had brought with him copies of pages from the red leather volumes in the castle, and since the reputation of the Order of St Anthony had gone before him, it was no surprise when his cell began to take on the appearance of a miniature apothecary. Neither did his excursions into the surrounding countryside attract any attention as he returned carrying small samples of plants and roots. Indeed it was only a matter of time before members of the curia began calling at his little cell with their own particular aches and pains, to which Henri benignly prescribed some of the lotions and ointments he made from the plant specimens.

If he saw a fair number of the members of the lower curia, he saw none at all of the scarlet clad Cardinals that swept haughtily past him discussing matters far too important to involve or even to acknowledge a mere Abbot from an obscure order. Henri contented himself with watching and listening.

One evening, when the bustling Vatican City quietened, Henri's thoughts turned to his Hashishin mentor, Yousef-al-Malik. He remembered how he had prepared himself for his task and subsequent death with calmness and an utter faith in his personal destiny. He remembered, too, how Yousef would justify the murder he was about to commit in the name of Islam, and the arguments he would put forth as to the requirement for Islam to triumph over the world.

Henri remembered all this with a certain amount of irony as he set about his task.

Methodically and with great care, according to the instructions he had brought with him, Henri prepared the paste of ground hemlock roots using a small pestle and mortar. He mixed the paste with a fiery spirit he had brought from the Cognac region to the north of their Sanctuary. Next he collected plums from the fruit trees lining the avenue approaching the Papal Palace. For several days he let these dry on wooden trays outside his cell window in the fierce Umbrian sun. When they had shrunk to a fraction of their previous size he took half a dozen and with a sharp knife slit them open and removed the stones. These he carefully replaced with some of the stiff paste he had prepared earlier. He carefully re-formed the dried plums and concealed the cut with a miniscule drip of wax. These he hid carefully under his bunk. The rest of the plums he soaked in the cognac spirit. He placed the bowl near to his cell door and waited.

It was not many days before the aroma of fermenting fruit and the fumes of the cognac began to attract people as they passed his door. The contents of the first bowl disappeared rapidly. Within days Henri was required to produce another batch. And it was not long before the effects of these succulent fruits began to have a dramatic result on the curia's bowel habits. Presently the entire Palace was alive with rumours of the wonderful laxative effects of Brother Henri's stewed plums. His skills as an apothecary were applauded. It was not many days before he received a request to attend His Holiness in the Papal apartments above him.

Pope Benedict XI was standing at the open window as a member of his curia bade Henri enter the room. The elderly Pope sat on a couch and indicated to Henry to do likewise.

'My courtiers tell me you prepare some wonderful fruits with some interesting properties!'

Henri smiled and offered a small plate with a dozen or so plums in the rich juice. Benedict took one and chewed on it, letting a little of the juice run down his chin. He was an old man even by Papal standards, and Henri marvelled at his thin stick like hands as they picked among the plate of fruit.

'I believe you know my personal chaplain, de Gothia?' Benedict said conversationally, his mouth continuing to chew.

'Indeed my lord, I fought with his nephew in the Holy Land' Benedict raised his eyes from the plate.

'A soldier?'

Henri smiled 'A Knight, Sir.'

Benedict nodded slowly. His eyes darted around the room whilst he continued to chew. The contents of his mouth were obviously causing some discomfort. Suddenly he held his hand to his mouth and spat out the handful of stones. Pope Benedict XI briefly became just another old man as he apologised to Henri whilst wiping his mouth.

'Pity these fruits do not come without the stones!' He opened his mouth to Henri to reveal a perfect set of pink, shining gums. The two laughed together.

It was not long before the Palace was rocking with laughter at the effect the fruit had had on the elderly Pope. Blessings and services were disrupted, as the Vicar of Christ needed quick access to his portable commode. Henri's fruits grew ever more popular. The sedentary life of many of the curia led to a permanent battle with their digestive systems when allied to the rich diet of the Papal Palace.

One day Henri noticed an increase in the tempo of Palace life. Members of the curia and Palace staff were rushing hither and thither, and preparations were being made for a grand banquet. An ambassador from King Philippe of France had been summoned in an attempt to heal the rift between King and Pope, caused both by the refusal of the King to allow revenues to leave France, and the widespread opinion that the death of the previous incumbent of the

Holy Office had been murdered on the direct orders of the King of France.

Abbot Henri was not involved in the visit, but he did receive a request from the Papal curia for some of his fruit for the Pope personally. He knelt long, as his father had done, on the cold stone floor of the cell. The moment Bertrand had spoken of was at hand. He retrieved the fruit, from which he had carefully removed the stones, and put six of them on a plate. Climbing the stairs he headed for the Papal apartments, but his way was blocked by the Pope's personal Swiss Guard. No amount of persuasion would gain Henri access to the Pope, so he had to be content in handing the plate to a courtier, giving strict instructions that the fruit was for the personal consumption of the Pope.

Henri had taken the precaution of providing a second plate of whole fruit, for Benedict's personal staff to prevent their surreptitiously dipping into their master's.

Henri retired to his cell, having watched the arrival of the French ambassador.

Later, much later, he was awakened by the sounds of running feet outside his cell. Donning his robe, he joined a group of worried-looking curia at the foot of the stairs to the Papal apartments. Benedict's screams could clearly be heard as various physicians and Cardinals from the Orsini and Colonna clans came and went, wearing ever more dismal expressions.

For Henri, the terrible sounds forced him to relive those moments in Baibars' encampment all those years ago. As he knelt on the stone floor of the cell, sounds of the old Pope's agony echoed throughout the castle. Various Orsini and Colonna Cardinals swept in and out of the Papal apartments all night, or gathered in small groups along the corridor; bitter rivals at court, but united in the belief that, yet again, this was somehow the work of Philippe IV.

It was several months before Henri once more rode back into his secret hideaway, to the intense joy of Eleanor, Raymond, now a rumbustious seven-year old, and a happily crawling Maria.

CHAPTER SIXTEEN

Some nine months after the death of Benedict XI, poisoned, it was widely believed, on the orders of King Philippe of France, the College of Cardinals was still struggling to elect a candidate. Although the smaller French faction that had flourished under Boniface held the balance of power between the warring Orsini and Collonna clans under no circumstances would the people of Rome accept a French Pope.

The heat of the summer had faded. The labourers on the estate were busy gathering crops and the fruit from the orchards. The weather merged one calm blue day into another, and slowly but surely the rich green hue of their secret world changed to golden straw and honey tones, bathed by the low autumn sun

Towards the end of September 1305 AD a small group of horsemen appeared at the entrance to the defile. They were not expected, and Henri had the drawbridge raised as a precaution. He watched from the battlements as the group, no more than five, cantered leisurely down the causeway. Even at a distance he could see they wore rough travelling clothes, and that their horses bore the foam and fleck of a hard ride. The riders' appearance was unkempt. Concerned rather than worried that they had found this place, Henri watched them through the iron grill of the mighty portcullis as they approached, gripping his sword as the tall leader swept back his coarse hood with a sudden gesture.

A dishevelled but unmistakable Bertrand de Gothia was revealed.

'Fine way to greet your father-in-law!' he called.

Eleanor shouted in pleasure. Henri cast his eyes over the Archbishop's retinue as the portcullis ground slowly upwards.

'Gilbert, what of Gilbert, Bertrand?' he cried.

'We'll talk about him later, but you need not concern yourself— he is at the court of Philippe IV as we speak,' replied Bertrand. Henri frowned but held his tongue.

Later, the three of them had retired to the library and Bertrand was poring over the red leather volumes, painstakingly completed by Eleanor, recording the progress of the work in the cavern. Eventually Bertrand laid his small eyeglasses down on the table and sat back.

'This will be my last visit for some considerable time,' he began. 'It will not be sufficient in future merely to travel incognito. The French court has spies everywhere, and it will be necessary to remain in France after next month.'

Henri glanced at Eleanor, who was regarding Bertrand with rapt attention. When Bertrand did not continue, Henri prompted. 'Next month?'

'Next month the Lateran council will elect a new Pope.'

Henri looked up sharply. *How could he know this in advance?...*

Bertrand continued, 'The new Pope will be French, and thus unacceptable to the people of Rome. Not only that, but his life would be at risk if he ever returned to Rome, so the Papal Residency would have to be in France under the jurisprudence and protection of Philippe IV.'

'Protection, Bertrand?' Henri said. 'Philippe was virtually at war with Boniface, and people have come to their own conclusion about the death of Benedict.'

A dry smile spread of Bertrand's face. 'Protection does not necessarily mean co-operation Henri. Gilbert, my own nephew, has had to remain at the Court of Philippe as personal surety to certain negotiations that I have been conducting of late.'

He rose and paced the room, his shadow dancing round the richly panelled walls in the light of the guttering candles, his face bowed and in darkness.

'Gilbert may be away a year or more until our plans can be executed. When the time is right, Henri, I will send for you and you will return to our sanctuary with Gilbert, for that you have my word. Until then we must keep our association and your family title a deadly secret, especially from the ears of Guillaume de Nogaret. He will, above all, have cause to suspect you of treason. History will judge me in a treacherous light my friend, of that I am certain, but if you take to your heart our recent conversations, and recall your time in Damascus, then you will have the strength and courage to understand the task you have before you, both of you.'

Henri nodded slowly. Yet another ambiguous message, full of portent, he sensed, not only for himself. 'You still haven't said what's happening to you next month,' he pressed.

Bertrand smiled wryly. 'Now that Philippe has his hostage, my nephew, Gilbert de Gothia, he will deliver his promise. As I am Archbishop of Bordeaux, which although part of France is under English fealty, the Italian Cardinals will have no difficulty in agreeing.'

'Agreeing to what?' said Henri exasperated.

'To having me elected as the next Pope, taking the name of Clement V.'

Eleanor' s firm voice, followed a moment of silence. 'We should kneel to thank God for His blessing.'

Bertrand nodded gravely as the three figures knelt together in the softly glowing room. He raised his hand to give the blessing. *'In nomini patri…'*

✠✠✠

In accordance with Bertrand's wishes it was to be almost two years before Henri met him again. Not that the inhabitants of the castle were short of news of him, for Eleanor had a constant flow of news from the outside world brought by visiting monks of their order.

The Order, having been ratified under the late Boniface VII, enjoyed the support of the clergy in France, which in turn was well politicised by Philippe IV. The parish priest's weekly homilies, whilst addressing the spiritual need of his flock, contained in no small measure Philippe's insidious propaganda against the Church, and, increasingly, against the alleged excesses of the Templar Order.

Some ten months after Bertrand had left the castle, and nine months into his Papacy, in July 1306, it was announced that Philippe had ordered the seizing of all Jews and their possessions within his Kingdom. Literally overnight every Jewish home and business was raided by his troops. Henri knew that after the Knights Templar and the Catholic Church, the Jews had been a substantial lender to the French Crown. It came as no surprise to find that all documents recording debts to the King were destroyed, whilst monies owing to the Jews were directed to the King's coffers. Eleanor's opinion was that it was 'A rehearsal, Henri, just a rehearsal. De Nogaret's hand is in this. By one event co-ordinated all over France in one night, Philippe has cancelled a third of his debts,' she said softly, linking his arm as they strolled in the heat of the day. Then she released his arm and turned to face him.

'Uncle Bertand has sent a message for you Henri. You must go to the prison at Toulouse. There is a man whom you may have met before as the Prior of the Templar preceptory of Montfaucon, near Perigeaux, called Esquiu de Florian'.

Henri nodded vaguely.

She continued, 'He was removed from office following various irregularities, but his bitterness and fury grew daily until it consumed him and he murdered his superior in an ambush one night after a failed attempt to regain his position. A character I think, not unlike Roger de Flor in Acre.'

She paused, and Henri watched her face. He seemed to see the narrow knife in her hand, and the final look of astonishment on Knight de Flors' face as it penetrated his brain.

She continued, her eyes cold as the leopard's. 'Esquiu de Florian is in prison in Toulouse, with an Italian informer called Arnolfo Deghi.' She held up her hand as Henri sought to interrupt. 'De Florian is attempting to obtain money and a pardon from the King of France in exchange for betraying the Rule of the Knights Templar. This bears all the hallmark of De Nogaret. Do not forget he originates from Toulouse, and attended the university there after the death of his parents. The man they have placed in the cell with him, Deghi, is de Nogaret's puppet and they are attempting to use Florian's evidence through his confession as to the heresy and witchcraft practiced by the Templars.'

'And what have I to do in Toulouse?' Henri asked.

'Escort de Florian and Deghi to Philippe IV's Court of Inquisition to be put on trial for their lives.' she said simply.

CHAPTER SEVENTEEN

The narrow streets of Paris around the Temple Preceptory echoed to the clatter of horse's hooves. It seemed half of Paris had turned out to witness the arrival of Grand Master Jacques de Molay of the Order of the Poor Fellow-Soldiers of Christ and of the Temple of Solomon, which was the official title of the Knights Templar. Accompanying him was a personal escort of sixty armoured knights, their helms and weapons burnished with a mixture of birdlime and sand until they shone like silver. Their snowy white surcoats, emblazoned with the crimson cross, made for a stirring sight that Paris morning. Not content with his sixty knights de Molay was also attended by his personal retinue of black robed squires and sergeants, who guarded a pack train of twelve horses carrying one hundred and fifty thousand gold florins, there was nothing "poor" about this Order. The entire procession wound its way through the narrow streets in an impressive display of invincible power and wealth.

De Molay had languished in Cyprus for ten years or more, beseeching each successive Pope to authorise and declare a fresh crusade to recover the Holy Land. Until the investiture of Clement V, of whose previous machinations he knew nothing, all his plans and pleading letters had been to no avail. Now he had received the Papal command to attend an audience with Clement at the Court at Poitiers.

Jacques de Molay knew that his time, and more importantly, the time of the Knights Templar, had returned. He had absolutely no intention of attending a provincial court; he was marching to Paris to stake his claim, before no less a personage than the King of

France himself. Jacques de Molay saw himself as the leader of the next Crusade.

He would have arrived a little less ostentatiously had he known that Philippe's lawyer, Guillaume de Nogaret, had been behind Clement's re-call of the Grand Master. De Molay was in fact more concerned that a movement begun by another priest and lawyer, Pierre de Bois, had given birth to an idea that could herald the end of his beloved Templars.

De Bois' document: *De Recuperatione Terrae Sanctae* cited the advantages of uniting the Hospitallers and the Templars in order to recover the Holy Land. Another Dominican priest, Ramon Lull had, with no sense of irony, suggested the head of this new Military Order, was to be called *Rex Bellator*, or War King, and should be King Philippe Le Bel of France. Furthermore Philippe should have control over the joint organisations considerable assets.

The Monastery and Church of St Germain de Pres had stood on the same site since the 6th century. Reputedly built by King Childebert 1st of the Franks, the church was built to house a relic of the True Cross brought from Spain in 542. It had been destroyed by the Norman invaders some two hundred years previously, but its new incarnation soared above the surrounding neighbourhood, rebuilt with the patronage of the current King of France.

De Nogaret deemed that his examinations of Escui de Florian would be better served if he involved the religious authorities from the start. Accordingly he had arranged for the inquisition to be held in the great hall of the Abbey of St Germain des Pres.

He had laboured behind the scenes to persuade the Palace of Justice that the trial of a man accused of murder should be held some distance from the scene of the crime, and before the Grand Inquisition. The Lord Chief Justice of Paris had questioned the setting of the trial with King Philippe, and to his surprise and embarrassment had been overruled. Now de Nogaret surveyed the magnificent court as he rose. Above the suspended candelabras the ornate wooden ceiling soared away into the darkness. Across the courtroom floor and opposite the judicial bench rose the tiered seats of the public gallery. Today they were full of the good burghers of

Paris, here to see a man on trial for his life. De Nogaret knew that as the trial progressed and the likelihood of the prisoner being sent to the scaffold increased so would the public's scramble for a place in the court.

Seated on de Nogaret's right was Guillaume Imbert, the Grand Inquisitor of France, appointed by the Pope, and personal friend of Philippe IV. On his left was Pierre de Bois, author of the document proposing the union of the Templars and Hospitallers. He nodded to the jailer at the rear of the court and a bowed, shackled figure was led to the dock.

'It is the duty of this court,' de Nogaret began, 'not only to try you for the murder of your superior from the Preceptory at Toulouse, but also to ascertain the nature of your allegations, the rumours of which have reached us from the jail at Toulouse.'

De Nogaret knew that in order to move against the Templars it would not be sufficient to prove that one or two errant knights had transgressed, no matter what the crime. Individuals could be rooted out and punished. For de Nogaret's plan, he had to prove that the very Rule of the Templar Knights encouraged heresy.

The Rule was of course not in written form, most Templars were illiterate including their Grand Master Jacques de Molay, but communicated to each knight orally at his initiation; perhaps there were no more than a dozen leading knights who knew the entire Rule. Each knight was forbidden to discuss it with anybody else. The secrecy of this situation made it ripe for rumours and hearsay. It was against this background that the Court sat in rapt attention at de Florian's evidence.

Esquiu de Florian was on trial for his life. On the first charge of Murder, if he was found guilty, his titled status would bring him the merciful attention of the headsman's axe. On the second charge, that of Heresy, hence his appearance at the Court Of Inquisition, he could expect nothing less than the terrible flames of the stake.

Earlier, in the gaol at Toulouse, de Florian's erstwhile cellmate, Deghi, had listened in fascination to de Florian's lurid account of his time at the Toulouse Preceptory. Deghi, a habitual thief, could reasonably expect to be flogged before being forced to join the King's army, with an altogether uncertain lifespan. He was a larger than life character, with whom de Florian would not normally have found himself in conversation. One day during their sojourn in the prison at Toulouse, Deghi was hauled from the cell by two burly gaolers. It was several days before the door clanged open again, and a bruised and beaten Deghi was thrown back into the cell.

De Florian knelt to attend to his companion, but was stopped in his ministrations by the silent appearance of a man of diminutive stature dressed entirely in black. He did not introduce himself, but spoke in a soft voice that caused a shiver to run through the Knight's body.

'You are from the Templar Preceptory I believe?'

De Florian merely nodded.

De Nogaret continued, 'There are certain actions within the Rule of the Templars that would be of great interest to my principal'. He shrugged. 'But here you are on trial for your life. So that even if we were to reward you for your information, you could not spend it from the gallows.'

De Florian rose to his feet, towering above the sinister little man, wishing fervently for a moment that he still had his sword.

'Then there is little point in my imparting my full knowledge of the Rule, if, as you say, only my executioners would benefit. But I doubt you have come all this way in your expensive attire merely to tell me that!'

De Nogaret feigned a sigh of resignation, and raised his hands expressively. 'A bargain then, a bargain, it always comes down to that in the end' He gestured for de Florian to sit, and with the battered Deghi still semi-conscious on the floor, he began to speak.

After the second day of the trial Guillaume de Nogaret left the Abbey of St Germain de Pres wearing a satisfied expression. He had spoken little, preferring to let the Grand Inquisitor perform his role before the Court. He had waited whilst de Florian had unburdened himself at length, and listened whilst the lawyer de Bois had conducted a detailed examination of the denials.

De Nogaret had cleared his throat and spoken quietly. 'You will be aware, Knight de Florian, that if a Catholic has no access to his priest he may, in those circumstances, confess his sins to another. The confession is witnessed by God and can only contain the truth.' He had received an affirmative nod from de Florian. De Nogaret's eyes had gone to the rear of the court, 'Call the witness!'

Arnolfo Deghi was led in to the court wearing new clothes, and with his hair carefully attended to. Flicking a guarded look at de Nogaret he took his oath in front of Inquisitor Imbert.

De Florian had risen to his feet to the consternation of his two gaolers, his face dark and furious. He recognised his cellmate from Toulouse:

'Sir, I must protest! Surely the Court would be beneath contempt if it were to take the word of a common criminal!'

Before he could continue, one of the gaolers clamped his hand over his mouth and forcibly wrestled him to the ground. For a moment de Florian fought, and the onlookers rose in confusion as the men spilled kicking and punching onto the court floor. Grand Inquisitor Imbert shouted his face furious, 'Remove the prisoner from my court! Take him to the cells and teach him how to behave!'

A still struggling de Florian was dragged from the court.

De Nogaret had sat silent and unmoved during the disturbance. For a moment he thought de Florian had over played his hand. However, as he watched the faces of the crowd in the public gallery after Deghi had taken his oath in front of the Grand Inquisitor, he nodded to himself satisfied. They were listening in rapt attention to Deghi's testimony.

Pierre de Bois had paced the courtroom floor, choosing his words carefully as he addressed Deghi,

'The oath you have sworn before this Court carries the penalty of death for perjury, you are fully aware of this fact, are you not?' Deghi nodded emphatically. De Bois paused for several long moments as the silence of the courtroom deepened. It was as if the breaths of the assembled crowd were being collectively held. He continued,

'In summary then you are prepared to swear before this court that during the confession of the accused, Knight de Florian, held in the cell at Toulouse, and witnessed by God Himself, certain practices now disclosed to the court took place in the Templar Preceptory, attended to and witnessed by Knight de Florian.

'All that I have spoken is true, Sir' affirmed Deghi.

A sigh went round the court with the realisation that a crucial part of the Trial had been reached. Surely now the burghers of Paris would be entertained by the flames of the stake.

De Bois raised his hand and the court was silent.

'Bring back the prisoner!'

De Florian was dragged across the courtroom floor. His gaolers supported him on either arm, his head hung low. A dribble of mucus and blood streamed from his battered face. He was barely able to stand unaided, and was propped up in front of the Judicial Bench.

De Bois returned to his seat and cleared his throat.

'Knight de Florian of the Templar Preceptory at Toulouse, we have heard in this court today, by virtue of your own confession to God, that in your time at the Preceptory, and with full knowledge and indeed participation of your Superiors, certain ceremonies were undertaken as part of the initiation of the Order; namely that you and members of your Order did spit upon the Cross of Jesus, and that you did indulge in lewd and immoral acts upon the altar of God Himself, by kissing the base of the spine in between the buttocks of a naked man whilst he was prostrate over the Altar. Further, as if these sacrileges were not enough, the severed head of a goat was worshipped, using the salutation of Bahomet. At this point perhaps I should inform the court that learned opinion has it that this title of Bahomet is a corruption of the word Mahomet, the prophet of the Infidels. We have documentary evidence linking the word with a Templar Prayer used in the Holy Land. I shall read these words to the Court taken from a Templar prayer.'

'And daily they impose new defeats on us: for God, who used to watch on our behalf, is now asleep, and Bahomet puts forth his power to support the Sultan.'

De Florian raised his weary head, 'My Lord, anybody with an ounce of intelligence would know that the Infidel do not worship idols of any kind—'

His words were cut off by a blow from his Gaoler.

De Bois continued silkily, 'But this is your confession to God, taken by the Court's good servant Deghi. Retraction of Holy Confession is Heresy.'

De Florian slumped, held only by his gaolers. De Bois nodded to the dark-robed scribe in the rear of the court, who hurried forward with the transcript of de Florian's confession. With a shaking hand de Florian scratched his mark on the velum. Collectively, the courtroom sighed. This was the moment that they had been eagerly anticipating. All the evidence, denials and accusations at last summed up in that one word, 'Heresy'. De Florian's head fell forward in defeat but not before he had looked towards de Nogaret, who gazed back coolly.

Grand Inquisitor Imbert rose and the court fell silent.

'On the charges of Heresy brought before this court, Knight de Florian, we find you guilty and sentence you to death at the stake. Further, as the sentence is to be carried out in the morning, I propose not to waste any more of the Court's time on the charge of murder, as its outcome would be pointless.' He dismissed the court.

In moments the room had emptied. Only de Nogaret sat for long moments, his face a mask.

Presently he rose, and holding a silk kerchief to his nose descended to the cells below the courthouse. His ominous authority sent the guard scuttling away as he entered de Florian's cell.

'Thank God you've come,' spluttered de Florian. 'I am but hours away from the stake.' De Nogaret motioned him to be seated.

'It is necessary for the machinery of state to proceed in the correct and legal manner, my friend. Tomorrow you will be taken to the Isle Des Juifs, the place of execution. You will be bound to the stake and faggots piled around you. But you need not worry. Only Grand Inquisitor Imbert can light the fire. He and I are to dine at the palace with King Philippe, and when you next see the Grand

Inquisitor I shall be accompanying him bearing the Royal Pardon. With, of course, the payment we discussed in gold.'

De Florian leant back against the hard cold walls in relief.

'Until tomorrow then.'

At dawn de Forian was taken to the gloomy, mist-shrouded Isle in the centre of the Seine and bound to a charred post set upon a raised stone dais. He protested little as the bundles of faggots were placed around him. The little courtyard fell silent as the crowds awaited the arrival of Grand Inquisitor Imbert. Moments passed and the crowd grew restless. De Florian's eyes switched to the door in the corner of the courtyard. It opened and Grand Master Imbert strode across the yard. Alone.

✠✠✠

De Nogaret hurried through the late afternoon's warmth, heading for the Royal Palace at Fontainebleau. His familiar diminutive form gained him rapid access to Philippe IV, and he found the King deep in conversation with his Chancellor, the Bishop of Narbonne, Bernard Saisset.

The Bishop glanced up at de Nogaret's approach, a fleeting look of frustration crossing his face. Philippe's upstart lawyer seemed to have a call on the King of France far above his station, the Bishop reflected. But Philippe nodded and beckoned de Nogaret closer.

'I bring news from England, Sire!' The lawyer began. 'Edward is dead, his son has succeeded as Edward II.'

Philippe raised his hands in triumph, a smile creasing his face. 'Praise God, at last, relief from the rapacious English!' He clasped his hands and knelt briefly in prayer. For a moment, their differences forgotten, three Frenchmen were united by the death of an English King who had for so long fought and harried their country. When he rose de Nogaret spoke for them all:

'Now, my Liege, the threat from England, a heinous and heavy drain on our country, is lifted. Edward's son, although now King of England, is no match for real men.'

The news had transformed the King. He strode vigorously round the room, and his voice boomed with confidence. Dismissing the Bishop he turned to face de Nogaret.

'Tell me of de Florian…' he began. The Bishop moved away, but he had heard enough. That night a figure slipped from the Bishop's palace and headed for the Papal Court at Poitiers.

That same Court, some weeks later in August 1307, rang to the harsh thrilling fanfare of the elite Royal trumpeters. On his Papal Throne, Clement V sat waiting to receive His Majesty, King Philippe of France. Known widely as Philippe the Fair, this was a reflection on his good looks rather than on any tendency to fairness in his dealings with others, as Clement wryly reminded himself.

As he waited in the draughty, vaulted Great Hall of his Palace at Poitiers, he surveyed its pitted walls, its uneven floor and its shabby furnishings with disgust. He thought of how he, himself, would oversee the building of the new Palace at Avignon. That would indeed be a fitting repository for part of his wealth, as, God willing, his plans over the coming years unfolded. He nodded graciously at the approaching figure of the King, and extended his hand bearing the Papal ring to be kissed.

Later in the privacy of the Court gardens, and with the sound of the river muting their conversation, Philippe began, 'A Knight has come to the Court of Inquisition held by Brother Guillaume Imbert.'

Clement noted wryly the King's use of the Dominican title; not Grand Master Inquisitor Imbert.

'He brings shameful evidence of the activities of the Knights Templar,' the King continued. 'The Templars have put their Order before the interests of Holy Mother Church. I doubt there are many who are not in debt to them,' he added sardonically. 'And, they have taken a secret oath to defend and enrich their Order by any means. They have communicated secretly with the Infidel, and indeed use a term in praise of Mahomet, whilst their secret initiation rites require novices to spit on the cross, and to deny Jesus. The Templars omit the words of consecration in the Mass, and it is through the treachery of the Templars that the Holy Land is lost.

Further, the use of satanic idols in their castles and Preceptories, in the shape of a bearded goat's head, and a cat, is widespread.'

Clement's face had become rigid, his eyes hard.

'Philippe, my son, do you give credence to any of this? Surely these are the rantings of the enemies of this most Holy Order?'

'I would not, Your Holiness, have travelled here in person to discuss mere rumours,' was Philippe's reply. 'There is a witness to the events I have described. He has been thoroughly cross examined by Pierre de Bois, and also by my Lawyer, de Nogaret.'

'Ah, of course,' murmured Clement. 'De Nogaret.' His eyes were lowered in apparent distress as he murmured that he would, of course, call a Papal enquiry in the remote chance that further evidence would be forthcoming.

He thanked Philippe for being a true son of the Church, and watched as the King and his entourage galloped away. Later, as he sat thinking, a knock on his door woke him from his reverie. He rose to greet his old friend.

'Bernard Saisset! Welcome to Poitiers.'

Saisset took the proffered seat.

'De Nogaret is almost ready sir, he has for some months been stockpiling chains and manacles, and daily a stream of spies report to him the levels of manning and readiness of the Preceptories. I cannot yet be sure of a date for his plans but I think we can count on early October.'

Clement regarded Saisset with affection.

'God knows, Bernard, you have served the Papacy well. Yet again you have put your life at risk for the one true Church.'

Bernard Saisset bowed his head in gratitude.

'I have one last request,' Clement continued. 'Go to Paris and seek out Brother Henri de Montfort, and my nephew, Gilbert de Gothia. Gilbert has been...a houseguest of Philippe these two years, but he is free to leave now.' He did not elaborate on this.

'Seek them and these other six knights.' He handed Bernard an envelope bearing the Papal seal. 'Seek them urgently. Tell them I require them in Poitiers within the week.'

✠✠✠

Henri, had slipped away from the Court at St Germain de Pres. Up until now he had retained his guise of Abbot Henri, merely escorting the two knights from prison at Toulouse. Upon his being presented, de Nogaret had glanced briefly at him without a flicker of recognition. It was a different story some days later when he had sought an audience with Philippe IV. Giving his full titles of Lord Henri de Montfort l'Amaury Prince of Armenia, Marquis de Gothia, to the courtier at the entrance to the Royal apartments, he had not long to wait. Rapid footsteps approached before the huge gilded doors were flung open. An astonished courtier could only look on in amazement as Philippe boisterously greeted Henri as a long lost friend. As the King engaged in a most un-royal-like bear hug, Henri reflected that it was indeed fortuitous that his own grandfather, Guy de Montfort, had been so pivotal in the life of Philippe IV's grandfather following the end of the Albigensian Crusades.

Philippe IV burst out laughing, a deep rich laugh, and his eyes twinkled. 'Not as an Abbot tonight, my dear de Montfort,' he gently chided. Henri smiled back.

'I have taken orders in truth, sire, I am an Abbot of the Order of St Anthony. However, as Your Majesty will undoubtedly appreciate, fine houses of God cannot run on prayer alone. I am here to collect my tithes from my estate at Montfort l'Amaury.'

'Of course, of course,' murmured Philippe.

'Tithes which I need to rebuild Castres following the local population's desecration of it due to my Grandfather's help in the Albigensian Crusades,' Henri continued.

'People's memories are long indeed, de Montfort.'

'My father had a low opinion of the Templars sir. In fact he blamed them for the loss of the Holy Land itself.'

Philippe glanced at him, unsure. 'You never took the cross?'

'I did indeed, sire,' Henri protested. 'As a Knight Hospitaller, I was pushed out of Acre by Khalil himself.' He allowed a trace of bitterness to enter his voice. 'The Templars did not save us then.'

Philippe watched him in silence for a long moment. 'There are many who share your thoughts, Henri. At this very moment I am instigating an enquiry on behalf of our Holy Father, Clement V, to ascertain the truth of the confessions of a Templar Knight with regard to the Templar Rule.' He hesitated, biting his lip, as if for a moment thinking perhaps that he had said too much. Then he placed his arm round Henri's shoulders and walked with him down the darkened corridor of the Royal Chateau at Fontainebleau.

He was murmuring into Henri's ear as they entered the Chapel of Louis VII that had been personally consecrated by the English Cardinal, Thomas a'Beckett. For many minutes the two men stood talking in muted undertones. At one point, Henri pulled violently away and his voice rose in protest. Then he became quiet, listening as the King's voice whispered on in the shadowed silence of the Chapel.

CHAPTER EIGHTEEN

It was late when an outwardly calm Henri retired to bed. In a sense much of what Philippe IV had disclosed in the sanctity of the Chapel had been expected, but as he tossed and turned in his apartments overlooking the Royal hunting forest of Fontainebleau he felt again the mysterious powerful force that had seemed to guide so much of his life; a force that seemed to have been with him since the dark days of Acre.

He drifted off to sleep and Eleanor came to him, a vision of beauty, calling him in whispers and behind her stood Clement, impassive, eyes boring into him. He sat up suddenly in the darkness, and knew with absolute clarity what he had to do.

He had of course previously observed Gilbert in one of the many courtyards; whilst from last night's conversation he knew that Gilbert had taken up the duties of hunt master to Philippe IV during his enforced stay. Henri had struggled to retain his composure as Philippe disclosed that His Holiness had sent him a witness of good faith, Gilbert de Gothia, a member of his own family, to undertake the inquisition on behalf of Clement.

As dawn broke Henri made his way to the great stables of the Chateaux. Hunting in the forests around the Palace was a daily occurrence, and Henri soon found Gilbert bellowing at a pair of hapless grooms. He had been careful to avoid a public greeting before, but now in the bustle of the yard, with noisy steaming horses milling around waiting for their morning exercise, he grasped Gilbert in delight and relief. Gilbert grinned openly at him, and then with a surreptitious glance to his left indicated caution.

Two figures sat immobile in the bustle of activity next to a stable door. They regarded Gilbert coolly. Henri drifted away feigning interest in his horse.

De Nogaret was not in the best of moods. He had been roused from his bed by a furious knocking on his door. Answering, he found a trembling figure. His anger had abated somewhat as he listened to his informant, and now he stood wrapped against the early autumn morning chill in a garret overlooking the assembled Hunt. His eyes narrowed as they found Gilbert de Gothia's figure near the impatient horses. The Abbot, Henri, who had accompanied Deghi and de Florian from Toulouse, was in close conversation with Gilbert. He knew of Gilbert's purpose here, indeed it was his own observation to Philippe IV that the wily Clement V would need some leverage to fulfil his promises that had led to Gilbert's enforced sojourn in Philippe's court. He watched as Abbot Henri wheeled and manoeuvred his horse, his face flushed with excitement as he conversed animatedly with Gilbert. He coolly formed the opinion that firstly Henri was a master horseman and secondly that his friendship with Gilbert de Gothia was a good deal deeper than this casual encounter would suggest.

Candles cast a flickering light over the room, whilst a log fire's dying embers shed a ruddy glow onto the faces of the room's occupants. King Philippe sat relaxed by the fire regarding the diminutive black clad figure before him. He waited as de Nogaret framed his statement; always the lawyer, always cautious. Some four years previously in February 1303, this had been the man who had bought charges against Boniface VIII; the man who had had the skill and cunning to take on the power and the might of the Holy Roman Church. So now the King waited.

'We have sufficient witnesses and evidence to proceed, Sire,' said de Nogaret simply. 'My plans are complete, my jailers await and the seneschals have been warned to expect orders on Friday the 13th October.'

Philippe nodded. He had expected nothing less. The fire burned lower and the room remained silent. He had waited for a long time for this moment, and he derived no small measure of satisfaction from it as he reviewed his options.

Clement V, the Pope himself, on French soil, and nervous of leaving it; was in fact, under Philippe's protection. Grand Master de Molay was even now planning his next Crusade, but crucially resident in France. And in Paris, not an hour's ride away, was de Nogaret, keeper of the Royal Seal and author of the grand plan about to unfold.

Philippe could almost see the Templar treasure being poured into his coffers. For a moment his mind allowed itself the luxury of imagining the treasures of the various Templar preceptories now to be his in no less than a week. He turned to de Nogaret. The dour lawyer continued.

'All in one day, sire, all on the 13th October. The inquisitors are waiting for their orders. We will have our confessions before Clement goes to bed that night.'

Philippe exhaled. The Confessions. Part of the Court of Inquisition's role was to extract confessions, as to the heretical acts undertaken, under torture if necessary. Confessions under duress were widely held to be the absolute truth, as God would allow true believers to speak only the truth. Naturally any knight that then retracted his confession became a relapsed heretic whose automatic fate was to be handed over to the secular authorities, to be burnt at the stake.

'Do it swiftly, make not any mistake, and do it for the King of France and the Holy Roman Church,' Philippe said simply. De Nogaret's face bore a flush of pleasure as he rose to his feet.

'I shall see to it immediately, your Majesty.' He bowed stiffly and walked calmly to the door. His hand on the ornate door handle he turned.

'Sire, there is one more small thing. The nephew of Clement, he who has been our, er, *houseguest* for two years, I saw him with the hunt this morning. He seemed very familiar with a Brother Henri, the abbot who accompanied De Florian and Deghi from Toulouse...' He paused, inviting comment.

'Abbot Henri?' The King looked puzzled. 'Oh yes, de Nogaret. That would be Lord Henri de Montfort l'Amaury. He was here only today. His grandfather and mine campaigned together long ago, he is a good and loyal servant.'

De Nogaret nodded, and made his exit. As he gently closed the doors behind him his eyes glittered, and his lips compressed. A name that had stalked his childhood, that of the man that had burnt his parents alive amongst hundreds of others in Beziers. Simon de Montfort, the most vicious evil commander of the Albigensian crusades in Southern France and Aragon. A man who had carried on his personal vendetta in the region long after a truce had been called. And now another scion of that accursed family was here, his trail only hours old. Abbot Henri, indeed. De Nogaret's legal mind turned the facts over. The de Montforts were strong allies of the papacy; and he had heard stories of their bravery in the Holy Land. His mind stalled. There was more, he knew. More—but what was it? A fact, something vital he was sure was eluding him.

He walked slowly down the portrait-hung corridor, his eyes unseeing. He ran over de Montfort's name again and again in his mind. Something of huge significance was teetering on the edge of his memory. He stood at the head of the beautiful staircase looking over the marble tiled floor. Above him a huge portrait of Philippe's wife, Isabella, loomed.

A woman!

Henri de Montfort had married, that he knew. He almost fell down the stairs in his excitement. Of course! He had married one Eleanor de Gothia, niece and goddaughter of Bertrand de Gothia, now His Holiness Clement V. Gilbert de Gothia, her brother, had been a hostage of Philippe these two years to ensure that the secret negotiations of Philippe IV and Clement V bore fruit. That was it! Eleanor had sent her husband to rescue her brother on the eve of de Nogaret's move against the Templars!

He went hurrying from the Porte Dore to the palace stables. It had been early morning when he had seen the pair, which meant that they had almost a day's start. There was no time to lose.

'Today,' Henri had whispered in Gilbert's ear, his voice almost lost in the stamping of the horses, steaming in the early morning chill. 'Today, Gilbert, you go home. Watch for my signal.'

He had wheeled away in an instant, excitement coursing through his body.

For much of the morning the hunt streamed in pack formation through the thinly wooded areas around Fontainebleau and Rambouillet. As each hog or deer was killed, either by arrow or hunting dogs, a small party of the hunt retinue would detach itself and set off back to the Chateau.

Henri sought Gilbert as the autumn sun reached its zenith. They slowed their horses down to a walk, ostensibly bored with the hunt and deep in conversation. Presently they lost the pack and were following a faint track through a glade. The two sour retainers who had accompanied Gilbert these last two months looked questioningly at Henri as he dismounted. Eyeing Gilbert he took from his saddlebag a bulging skin of wine and two goblets. Gilbert, taking his signal, dismounted, and the two took seemingly long draughts from the goblets. They were large pewter goblets and, when being drained, quite covered a man's face. Making a show Henri wiped his lips with the back of his hand, and made to offer Gilbert a further draught from the skin.

'We should share our wine, Brother Henri,' rebuked Gilbert. 'These men have become separated from the party and have brought no refreshments.'

Feigning a show of embarrassment, Henri half filled the two goblets. With perfect split second choreography he and Gilbert offered them to the two retainers, who took them with surly thanks raising them to their lips.

They had had no refreshment since early dawn. Greedily they drank, heads thrown back. The poison acted instantly as they slumped heavily to the ground.

Wasting no time Henri and Gilbert leapt onto their horses. 'Paris, quickly, one last call at the Preceptory then we ride for Home,' Henri shouted, spurring his horse down the glade.

By mid-afternoon the two horses were walking sedately down a Paris street towards the Templar Preceptory. Grand Master de Molay was in residence, and had only just returned from a royal funeral. He had been acting as pallbearer for the body of Princess Catherine, the dead wife of Philippe IV's brother Charles of Valois. He had been all day in the company of Kings, Dukes and Archbishops, and was tired, so it was with some reluctance he agreed to meet Henri.

'Grand Master, we must speak alone.'

Henri indicated the ranks of courtiers and sergeants, waiting until a weary de Molay had motioned them away. Henri fumbled under his garment and produced a small seal, which he presented to the Grand Master.

'Know this; I am on Clement's business, sir. Ask me not how I know, but your train has arrived with one hundred and fifty thousand gold florins from Cyprus.'

De Molay's eyes narrowed, but he remained silent. Henri continued speaking softly as horses and men milled around them out of earshot.

Some time afterwards two riders left the Preceptory gates. They sat astride their two horses, looking casually up and down the scarcely populated street. Clatters of hooves at one end of the street made both riders look in that direction. Guillaume de Nogaret, mud-splashed and filthy from his ride from Fontainebleau, raised his voice, a deep powerful voice that carried the length of the street.

'Arrest them! Arrest them in the name of the Inquisition, a gold florin for the man who brings them down!'

The group of riders escorting de Nogaret spurred their horses down the street, scattering the bystanders. Promptly the two riders in front of the Templar Preceptory dug in their heels and fled in the opposite direction. De Nogaret's deep voice could be plainly heard urging on his guards to even greater efforts as they pursued the two horsemen.

Peace reigned once more as the street returned to its quiet afternoon. A little while later, the huge double doors of the Preceptory opened again, and a creaking cart piled high with the stable's waste of straw and stinking manure turned into the street. Henri rode alongside the groaning cart. Considering it seemingly carried just straw and manure it was protesting loudly from every creaking joint. Gilbert glanced at him from the driving seat, his eyes twinkling behind the mask of flour and grains that covered his face. His left hand holding the reins was blackened, and in his other he hand carried a small bell. He grinned painfully as his mask cracked. Henri shook his head in amusement at Gilbert's predicament.

'You should be safe getting out of Paris, my friend. In a day or so I'll send some brothers to escort you, the journey will be long, but you must get to La Val Dieu. I will ride for Chateau Bezu tonight to warn them. God speed, Gilbert, Eleanor awaits both of us.'

Without further ceremony he galloped off, his horse's hooves echoing on the cobbles.

He drove his horse hard that night, his mind was as alive and active as his mount's flying hooves. He thought of Gilbert plodding slowly southwards, his face smeared with a pox-like paste, and he smiled in the darkness. He thought too of his other six knights carrying Bertrand's letters to various Preceptories. Templar Preceptories that by now should have begun to move their treasures to the Monastery of La Val Dieu. He laughed out loud in the rushing cool night air as he imagined de Nogaret's face after the raids. With the majority of the French army tied up guarding prisoners and empty Templar fortresses, the roads of France and Aragon should be safe for a few weeks to come.

CHAPTER NINETEEN

Friday the thirteenth, October 1307 dawned clear and bright. De Nogaret had personally taken charge of the assault on the Paris Preceptory. It had all been so ridiculously easy. Bearing the King's letters and seals, and invoking the name of God and the Holy Roman Church, they had demanded the doors be opened to a small group of Court Officials. The moment the huge doors had swung open, de Nogaret's heavily armed group of men had ridden straight into the Preceptory courtyard.

Now, after several hours, the sixty knights and attendant squires and sergeants stood chained against the walls. The air rang with shouts of protested innocence, of lives devoted to God in the pursuit of the Infidel. De Molay alone stood silent and glowering, his fall the more astonishing. Only the day before a pallbearer for the body of the wife of King Philippe IV's brother, and now shackled as a common criminal whilst this weasly faced lawyer supervised the erection of various instruments in the courtyard.

An unforeseen element had been the inability of the Preceptory cellars to hold all the prisoners, so that the proceedings would have to take place in the open air. De Nogaret had the huge gates barred to the assembled seething mob, greedy for sensation in the street outside. After a while he left the yard and mounted the stairs to the first floor balcony, the better to observe the proceedings. In no particular order a tall knight was brought from the walls, escorted by two black clad members of Imbert's Inquisition. Roughly and without ceremony they flung him down on an iron bedstead arrangement shackling his feet, arms and torso. Bizarrely his feet overhung the short bed. Guillaume Imbert motioned with his hand,

and a small writing desk was brought to the side of the terrified man. Smoke briefly hid the little scene as silence descended on the courtyard, and a charcoal brazier was lit. Kneeling at the bedstead, one of Imbert's assistants delicately anointed the knight's feet with oil.

Imbert began. 'Have you ever denied Christ as part of the initiation ceremony of the Knights of Jerusalem?'

The shackled figure shouted his denial.

'Have you ever been ordered to spit on the crucifix or worship an idol of a bearded head and a cat?'

Again, the protestation of innocence.

'We have heard that during the secret Templar ceremonies, held after dark, new members of the Order indulge in the Osculum Infame or kiss of shame, you kiss the Prior on his mouth, or his navel, or below his spine, would you agree?'

Again the hoarse, 'No!'

Imbert laid his quill down with a resigned look. 'God will protect the innocent from the pain,' he remarked and nodded to the two figures at the foot of the bed. The coals in the little brazier were now glowing and virtually smokeless. It was pushed under the knight's feet. His screams echoed around the courtyard as the oil thinned and dripped in the heat. Presently it began to heat and give off wisps of smoke. From his writhing heels blackness and blistering began to spread up the whiteness of his feet. The Knight's screams were indescribable. Several prisoners retched against their chains. Only when his feet were completely blackened was the brazier pulled away. It did not stop the screaming as the hot oil continued to cook the wretched man's feet. Imbert resumed the questioning.

Allowing himself a thin smile of satisfaction de Nogaret turned and went into the Preceptory. All around him, oblivious to the sounds from the courtyard, soldiers were carrying all manner of paintings, hangings, precious objects and items of furniture. He grasped a burly sergeant and questioned him.

'What of the gold? And the jewels we know are here? All I observe your men carrying are the trinkets of a great house.'

The sergeant shook his head and indicated his men were now searching the furthest outbuildings of the Preceptory. Frowning, de Nogaret continued his own meticulous examination of the buildings. For such a wealthy order he had expected more gold and silver. Much more... King Philippe had remarked on more than one occasion that when he had to borrow from the Templars they had been able to supply the money extremely quickly. Still it was early days yet, he mused, and dismissed the nagging worry from his mind.

It was some time later that the truth began to dawn on de Nogaret, as he inventoried the contents of the Preceptory. It was when he remembered the futile chase of the two knights from the gate of the Preceptory the day before the raid that everything began to make sense. His band of soldiers had eventually overtaken the fleeing knights, and forced them to halt. In an act of fury and frustration at discovering two sergeants who claimed to be merely exercising their mounts, Guillaume had them thrown into the inquisition dungeon. He went quickly to the stables. As with everything in the Preceptory they were orderly, and beautifully kept. All the horses' tack, gleaming and polished, were suspended from the walls, and a selection of working carts were reversed in ordered rows against a wall. One was missing. Guillaume de Nogaret stood in its empty berth and nodded slowly to himself.

Miles away the missing cart creaked alarmingly as it laboured up the slopes of the Puy de Dom on its journey south. Five other Brothers of the Order of St Anthony, who now accompanied the protesting cart, had joined Gilbert. Bales of cloth and barrels of ale had replaced the straw, but it still sagged and swayed at the limits of its capability. Gilbert and two others sported the flour pox mix, as they called it, whilst the remainder of the black-robed monks tolled small hand bells. The little group was left quite alone as it journeyed south.

Guillaume stood for a long time in the empty stable. His anger had abated somewhat and now his cool legal brain was analysing his problem. Not for nothing had the Templars been called the bankers of Europe. They had invented a system of debits and credits that did away with the need to transport gold the length and breadth of Europe. Merely depositing a sum with one Templar Preceptory meant that, with suitable documentation, an equivalent sum could be withdrawn at another Preceptory in a different town, or, for that matter, country. Musing quietly to himself he made his way to de Molay's quarters.

The large, well-lit room was quiet, and many of the more portable valuables had been removed. In a corner, its surface splashed with light from the leaded French glass windows, stood a lectern. Guillaume fingered its sloping surface thoughtfully. Turning, he observed a double row of oak shelves, quite empty, above it. He minutely examined the shelves' surface. There in the faint dust he could see the outlines of many books or ledgers. That was it! He had it now. He had been using his time as if he were a frantic hound, trying to locate hidden vaults and rooms. The key would be in the missing volumes. He hurried from the room to draft another question to be put to the screaming knights in the courtyard below.

By the end of the first week, Grand Inquisitor Guillaume Imbert stood before Philippe IV. He clutched in his hand a sheaf of manuscripts.

'Fifty two signed confessions, your Majesty.' He bowed slightly.

'Sixty knights were held, were they not?' questioned Philippe.

The man before him nodded and smiled dryly. 'One died under questioning, whilst seven recanted their confessions, claiming they had only confessed to prevent further agony. They were burnt at the stake immediately. As relapsed heretics the law demands this,' he added simply.

Philippe nodded. This was welcome news indeed. The Papal court at Poitiers had erupted in fury at the arrest of the Order, reporting direct to the Pope. Philippe had cunningly recalled his conversation with Clement only a month before, when he presented the rumours of the heretical Order of Templars. Clement had said "My son, you must look into their deeds with diligent care, and report to me what you make of them." The fury of Clement, in public at least, had led to the suspension of his Grand Inquisitor

Imbert. Now, clutching his evidence, Philippe had, with a great show of piety, taken the confessions to the Papal Court. By November 22nd, just over a month since the arrests, Clement V issued a bull; "*Pastorallis preeminentae*", praising the actions of Philippe IV, and recognising him as a True Son of the Church, and loyal Defender of the Faith.

Clement's bull formally recognised the truth of the charges against the Templar Order, and commanded all Christian kings to move against the Order in their own kingdoms.

✠✠✠

Eleanor's finger traced gently the entries in the ledger before her. It was, of course, identical to the one her brother had rescued from Acre. But instead of wisdom and the knowledge of herbs, these additions to the library at La Val Dieu contained the inventory of two hundred years of financial investment and acquisition. Apart from housing the well-organised accounts of the assets continually arriving deep within the cavern, this well-lit turret room was her nerve centre, it housed her records of the Knights of St Anthony's mighty financial empire. It was an empire that only a handful of people would ever be aware of; an empire that would affect and guide the future of the most powerful Church on earth.

Henri turned from his reverie. He had been mesmerised by the currents, flows and eddies around the stone pillars of the Pont St Benezet at Avignon. Secretly summoned from La Val Dieu by Clement V, he had waited patiently. The bridge was indeed a miraculous structure, and he had surveyed its twenty-two arches from the bank leading to the fortress of Phillipe le Bel. That such a narrow bridge could remain upright against the powerful flow of the river was astonishing. As he watched, a sodden tree trunk, a victim of a storm further up the river, maybe as far as Lyons, struck the pillar on which he stood. He felt the vibration as the current built up behind the log. Then with a rasp and a shake it was driven down one side of the pillar and released to continue its journey to the Mediterranean.

As he turned away, a monk approached, head bowed. Henri, in recognition, made as if to kneel.

'No, Henri, we are being watched, my friend,' Clement said.

The two men leant casually on the stone parapet, the ripple of the current masking any conversation. Henri gave Clement V a brief summary of all that he had done for the last six years. Even after all this time the cavern was full of unloaded carts full of Templar treasure. Eleanor had had to take on additional bookkeepers, and the metallurgists had resorted to smelting much of the precious metal at night. A permanent haze of smoke was beginning to hang over the Forest of Railesse. Henri described the amounts of oak needed for racking in the long corridors underground, and the problems of disposing of the ash from the furnaces after each smelting. He attempted briefly to describe the amounts of gold and jewel encrusted artefacts he now held, but found it difficult to convey the idea of the vastness of the accumulated treasure.'

'At the rate of progress, sire, it will be another two years to clear the backlog.'

Clement nodded with deep satisfaction. 'Yes, your task is indeed an onerous one, Henri. But as you struggle to record our fortune, de Nogaret is reaching a frenzy of activity. He has had the King appoint Philippe de Marigny as the Archbishop of Sens against my wishes, and as a result fifty-four knights have been burnt at the stake in Paris over the last two years. Thank God, as the flames burnt and blistered their skin, not one thought to save his life and reveal the whereabouts of the records of the Treasures of the Knights Templar. Not one, Henri!'

Clement watched Henri's eyes grow sad at the fate of these brave Knights. Then Henri crossed himself, his eyes hardening. Clement continued, 'That fifty four men should choose to die in that manner without a thought of saving themselves, does it not leave you with a sense of our destiny, Henri?' He dabbed a silk kerchief at his eyes. 'It is indeed God's Will, nothing less. King Philippe is sated at present. He has sold off numerous holdings and lands. Of everyone involved I think only de Nogaret has an inkling of the true extent of our subterfuge, and of how much we have prevented falling into their hands.'

Henri absorbed his words. He met infrequently with Clement, and then it was always done clandestinely. Eleanor had told him that Clement had moved to the Dominican priory of Avignon. He waited for confirmation of her words.

'We will build a new Papal palace here to rival anything we had in Rome and it will be built under the protection of King Philippe himself,' Clement grimaced wryly. 'Here at the centre of Europe, at the first bridge of the mighty River Rhone, we will build in veneration of God, and with the Order of St Anthony not too far away, it will be the basis of that which I discussed with you some years ago.'

Clement paused as he watched the swirling eddies of the river below. His face betrayed his inner struggle as he spoke lower, and in a resigned tone.

'History will judge me harshly, Henri, as I have intimated. Our journey transcends generations to come and the destruction of the Infidel is undoubtedly a task too much for one man's lifetime. I believe, I hope, my actions will one day be regarded as the cornerstone of our achievement, but I fear I will be called to judgement for those actions. On the other hand, Henri, no such fate awaits you or your descendants, for you are invisible, an unknown force without which we could not contemplate the fight to come. Guard the secret well, Henri. Guard it with your life.'

Henri nodded silently. It was his way. The Pope's desires and wishes were transmitted orally only. He clasped Clement's hand and turned to go.

'One last thing, my Henri.'

Henri turned to look into Clement's implacable eyes.

'It is almost over now,' the other man continued. 'De Molay and de Charnay are to be publicly paraded in front of Notre Dame. King Philippe and Guillaume Imbert want their confessions to be made in public. You must go, but do not let anybody recognise you.'

Clement bent to Henri's ear. His words lost in the river breeze. At one point Henri recoiled, but Clement gripped his arm fiercely.

'In this you must not fail; listen to de Molay.'

In an instant he whirled and was gone. His robed figure joined other several dark clad brothers at the end of the bridge. He did not turn round.

CHAPTER TWENTY

Henri had, with hundreds of tense and expectant Parisians, waited patiently since dawn on that chilly grey March morning. The air in the square hung heavy with the scent of cut pine, and rang to the sound of hammers and saws. Since first light carpenters had toiled to erect a huge platform in front of Notre Dame. Here the four remaining Knights of the Temple of Jerusalem were publicly to confess their crimes, and the profanities regularly performed by their Order. Over the last few years public suspicion had been growing that the brutal suppression of the Order had more to do with Philippe Le Bel's greed for their riches, than anything else. De Nogaret had arranged the public confession in order to quell the public's increasing hostility to the persecutions. De Molay, now approaching seventy, had confessed all that had been put to him. This was partly from his terror at the thought of more of the horrendous torture planned for him if he didn't comply, but at the back of his mind was the thought that if he could somehow put his case directly to Pope Clement rather than to Philippe IV and de Nogaret's prosecutors, then the whole misunderstanding could be cleared up. Clement, of course, had no intention of meeting the Grand Master face to face. Henri already knew that through a process of bargaining, the four knights had agreed to accept a lifetime's imprisonment in return for their lives.

Henri pondered on Clement's last words as he slowly inched his way to the front of the crowd. Usually his monk's habit and his greying stubble was enough to persuade the surliest of Parisian to make way, although he occasionally heard a muttered curse as to the arrogance of the man of God. Presently he stood at the foot of the wooden staircase leading to the platform. A disturbance at the back of the restless crowd drew his attention, and shortly the four knights, resplendent in fresh snowy white robes with their famous crimson cross patees, escorted by grim faced members of King Philippe's personal Guard, arrived at the foot of the platform. Their humiliation was there for all to see as, weighed down with chains and manacles; the frail elderly men grasped their way up the wooden steps to the platform. Presently they stood shoulder to shoulder gazing out over the crowd. Not one of them bowed his head. Grand Inquisitor Imbert stepped to the edge of the balcony above, and raised his arms. The crowd fell silent, men lifted their faces to the platform, and women stilled impatient children.

'Burgers of Paris, you are gathered here today, under the auspices and guidance of King Philippe IV, finally to lay to rest the rumours and half-truths surrounding the fall from grace of the once mighty Knights Templar. You will hear the confessions of heresy and immoral practices that have alone caused their downfall. Not through the greed of our mighty King, but through their own monstrous deeds. Listen carefully, my friends, for you shall not hear their voices again. They will leave this place for a lifetime of imprisonment in atonement for their sins.'

He stepped back and motioned a guard toward de Molay. A rough shove sent the silver-haired Grand Master to the edge of the platform. For a moment he said nothing as his rheumy eyes surveyed the crowd. He gripped the rail in front of him and began, his voice frail but gaining in strength.

'I think it is only right at so solemn a moment, when my life has so little time to run, that I should reveal the deception which has been practiced on you all, and speak up for the truth.'

An expectant tremor ran through the crowd. Henri watched as Imbert's face paled at de Molay's words. The Inquisitor made a sudden movement, but there was nothing he could do. De Molay continued. 'Before heaven and earth and with all of you here as my witnesses, I admit that I am guilty of the grossest iniquity. But the iniquity is that I have lied in admitting to the atrocious charges levelled against this Holy Order. I declare, as I stand before you, that the Order is innocent of all mortal Sin. There has been no heresy. The purity and Saintliness of the Order is beyond question.'

A low murmur ran through the crowd. This was not what they had been told to expect. In defying the Grand Inquisitor these must surely be the words of a condemned man. And a man on the point of death would not lie. Silence fell again in the vast square, broken only by the quickly stifled cry of a child. De Molay's thin voice, gaining strength, continued.

'I have indeed confessed that the Order is guilty, but I have done so only to save myself from the most horrific tortures. Others of my dear brother knights who have retracted their confessions have been led to the stake, yet the thought of dying is not so awful that I shall confess foul crimes which have never been committed. Life is offered to me, but at the price of infamy. At such a price, life is not worth having. I do not grieve that I must die, if life can be bought only by endangering my immortal soul.'

Inspired by de Molay's words, Geoffrey de Charnay stepped forward, further to proclaim the innocence of the Order. An angry crowd, believing the words of a condemned man, and having had their long-held suspicions of the complicity of the French king, confirmed drowned his words.

Frantically the guards and officers of the Inquisition bundled the four Knights down the steps. Henri caught a glimpse of Imbert's face suffused in dark anger. At the foot of the stairs, de Molay and de Charnay were roughly stripped of their Templar robes before being bundled into a crude tumbrel. A crowd followed as best it could down the narrow Paris streets to the river. There the two men were thrown roughly into the bottom of a riverboat, which cast off and headed downstream. The crowd milled uncertainly, but several jumped into other craft and followed. Henri did likewise, caught up in the macabre pursuit of the two condemned men.

A little island in the centre of the river called 'Isle des Juifs' was their destination. Without further ceremony the two men were chained to two posts, and their executioners set about stacking bundles of wood around them. Henri splashed ashore with about thirty Parisians who had come to witness the spectacle. He saw with a sense of creeping horror that the bundles of faggots and twigs were a mix of cured and green wood, specially chosen to produce a slow-burning fire of intense heat that would slowly roast the men from the ground up, in order to prolong their lives and agony for as long as possible. Without any further delay, flaming brands were thrust into the piled wood. The flames took a hold of the dried bundles, causing the green twigs to splutter and begin to smoulder. The two men were enveloped by swirling white smoke. They began to cough; great, harsh racking coughs as they fought desperately for air. The heat intensified as the flames licked upwards towards the men. Their desperate, gasping coughs were replaced by their screams of agony as the first flames began to lick at their feet. The two men's agonised features swirled and swam in the heat, and they strained at the chains holding them. The dancing flames took hold of the cotton shifts they had been wearing after their armour had been removed, and their screams became one. Then de Charnay's head fell forward and he was silenced. As the flames caught at his silver hair, de Molay cried out, his face twisted into a rictus of suffering,

'Within a year I call unto King Philippe to meet me in heaven to answer these charges. I call upon Pope Clement V to meet me there also.'

The small crowd grew silent as the flames engulfed the two men. Several of the crowd sank to their knees in prayer. Here had died most horribly two innocent men, that was certain. Later, as the flames flickered lower, individuals darted forward and picked still smouldering bones from the ashes. They wrapped them in anything they could find and scurried away.

Henri lingered long after the last of the crowd had gone, unable to tear himself away from the burnt and twisted remains of the brave Knights. His mind drifted to another place and time; a time when he had fought alongside men like these against a common foe. Men he had depended upon, and on whom he could trust with his life. Granted authority from the highest source in the world for his current undertakings, he could only wonder as he turned sadly away.

Henri now had two final tasks entrusted to him by his father-in-law and friend Bertrand de Gothia. Two tasks he would relish.

CHAPTER TWENTY ONE

De Nogaret bent once more to the open volume before him. It was late, and the light was fading as fast as his frustrations were increasing. For six months following the execution of de Molay and Charnay he had scoured the length and breadth of France, searching ransacked Preceptories and Castles. Granted King Philippe was highly pleased with the sale of lands and valuables that the dissolution of the Templars had brought to his coffers, and for the moment he was sated. But de Nogaret was reluctantly beginning to realise that something was wrong, very wrong. He scratched his ribs, not for the first time that day. In fact his entire body was beginning to itch like the devil. He stood up; his concentration ruined, and cast off his tunic. He saw the angry red weals stretching across his body and bellowed angrily for his bath to be run. Later, in the darkness of his apartment, he tossed and turned, scratching frantically. He was bathed in sweat, and he had a raging thirst.

Over the next few days he found he could not bear the feeling of clothes on his body, and ran around naked as if possessed. His servants cowered in fear at his rage.

By the fourth day his fingertips had begun to blacken and rot, but he continued to scratch frantically with the putrefying stumps. He was unable to close his staring eyes, and his bloated tongue hung grotesquely from his mouth. His servants belatedly recognised the onset of St Anthony's Fire, and sought out one of the Monks of the Order. Abbot Henri's timely arrival was seized upon with considerable relief. He went to de Nogaret's room and having drawn the heavy curtains, seating himself in the gloom next to the victim's sweating, writhing form. Insisting on the servants leaving the room, he knelt and prayed for the soul of Guilaume de Nogaret.

De Nogaret could not drink, for his tongue was horribly swollen and beginning to blacken, but Henri administered a goblet of liquid to his patient's grateful thanks. The diluted saliva from a rabid dog which was contained in it gave de Nogaret an ever more raging thirst, which he could not assuage without Henri's help.

For two days Henri sat quietly as his patient tossed and turned, moaning incoherently. Then he rose and drew the curtains, flooding the apartment with light and provoking a scream of pain from de Nogaret. He crossed to the bed and holding de Nogaret's head, gently, offered a small goblet to his lips. A little of the liquid dribbled past de Nogaret's swollen tongue. Henri stood up and swept his hood back. Against the light of the windows de Nogaret could see only a dark silhouette.

'Extract of Belladonna, my friend. Shortly you will be unable to move a single muscle of your body. You will remain in agony from now until your last breath, my job is done.'

His assassin turned abruptly and left the room. De Nogaret lay still, his eyes staring blankly, his tongue thrust out the length of a man's hand.

Pont Sainte Maxence November 29th 1314

Now there remained Henri de Montfort's final task, entrusted to him by the late Pope Clement V. Clement himself had died, a month after de Molay's execution, almost certainly poisoned by de Nogaret.

Now Henri's hand strayed to the tiny sheath in his rich leather boot, as, just before dawn, he headed for the Royal estate at Fontainebleau.

Using his new title of Lord Henri, Grand Prior of The Order of St Anthony, he had little difficulty in persuading the stable hands he was a guest of honour for that morning's hunt. He waited patiently. Presently the cobbled yard rang to the clatter of many hooves as the Royal entourage assembled. Philippe stood in his stirrups, his face flushed and arrogant as he surveyed the assembled knights. His eyes fell on Henri and he nodded in recognition, a smile touching his lips.

'You are most welcome to grace us with your presence, de Montfort, I was not aware you were at l'Amaury' this time of year.' His horse fidgeted, and he whirled away before Henri could reply.

The hunt streamed from the Chateaux walls, huge thundering chargers, their breath like clouds on the cold air, the jingle of chain mail mixing with the calls of the horns.

The quarry was elusive that morning, and before long, King Philippe, always in the lead, was accompanied by just two knights, one of whom was Henri. Entering a heath of low scrub and stunted trees, Henri bent forward in the saddle. In his right hand he held the bolo of knotted rope and heavy weighted stones. Keeping it shielded from the King's view he whirled it briefly, then, with a fluid movement, flicked the spinning rope under his horse's neck, towards the royal mount.

The whirling rope and weights wrapped themselves around the forelegs of the King's horse, and in an instant horse and rider crashed to the ground. Henri was at the fallen King's side at once. He glanced up. The second knight had turned and was galloping back. Shouts behind him warned of the rest of the hunt's approach.

Reaching down, Henri extracted the slim blade from his boot. Cradling the King's dazed head in his arms, he placed the point of the blade in his ear. His smile held Philippe's eyes for a second, and then he rammed the blade home. The King's eyes widened fractionally. Then he grew limp. Henri withdrew the narrow blade and re-sheathed it. Scooping up a handful of earth, he pushed some of it into the King's ear to stop the flow of blood. Quickly he smeared the rest of it over the King's face so that it looked like the result of the fall. He pushed the bolo out of sight as the other rider galloped up.

'The King is badly hurt,' he shouted. 'We must get him back to the Chateaux.'

Dusk was falling as the other huntsmen arrived, and anxious, exclaiming figures came running to surround the King's lifeless form. Henri the assassin melted into the darkness.

✠✠✠

Dieu le veut

EPILOGUE

In 1382, through his mistress Beatrice de Montfort, Albert I Duke of Bavaria became Grand Prior and set up the Order's Grand Priory at the Monastery of Schyren. The Counts of Shyren who became the Wittlesbach family were one of the nine original Anthonine families who fought together at the battle of Poitiers in 732 AD.

Until the death of Maximillian III, Elector of Bavaria, in 1777, the Grand Priors were always under the protection of one of the Electors of The Holy Roman Empire, hence the Order's Arms of the Blue Tau Cross of St Anthony superimposed upon the double-headed eagle of the Holy Roman Empire, its motto *Dieu le veut* [God wills it] was the cry of the people at the declaration of the first crusade by Pope Urban II at the Council of Clermont in 1095. Following Maximillian's death, The Hospitaller Order Of St Anthony was subsumed into The Knights of The Hospital of St John of Jerusalem, commonly known as the Knights of Malta .

On December 11th 1917 General Allenby accompanied by Major General Sir Raymond Mountford, Knight Grand Commander of St Anthony, entered Jerusalem as conquerors for the first time since it was captured by Saladin in 1187. On January 17th 1918 they celebrated Mass with the Anthonines on the Temple Mount .

The Knights of St Anthony and its nine families continue to be headed by a direct descendant of Henri and Eleanor de Montfort and meet on January 17th at noon every ten years.

On January 17th 1991, on the eve of The Gulf War, the nine Commanders of the Knights of St Anthony met at noon at the church of St Mary Magdalene at Rennes le Chateaux.

But that is another story...

Henri de Montfort Father's line

Aumery de Montfort III   Robert de Beaumont   Count Balien   Duke John
Count of Evereux   Earl of Leicester   of Ibelin   Komnenos
        /   /   /   /
Simon III de Montfort   **m** Amice   Balien **m** Marie Komnenos
Earl of Evreux   Countess of Leicester   of Ibelin   Queen of Jerusalem
        /   /
Guy de Montfort - Castres   **married**   Helvis of Ibelin
                                        /
Count Philippe I de Montfort l'Amaury Lord of Tyre----**married**----
(**1**) Eleanor de Courtney   (**2**) -Princess Maria St Gilles of Armenia
            /
      (1) Count Philippe II de Montfort Castres
(2) Jean Lord of Tyre   (3) Humphrey Lord of Beirut and Toron

(4) Henri St Gilles de Montfort l'Amaury-Castres (The Lion)
Prince of Jerusalem, Armenia and Cyprus
Count of Tripoli, Toron, Tyre Antioch and Beirut
Knight Commander of The Hospitaller Order of St John of Jerusalem

Married

Marquise Eleanor de Gothia

Henri De Montfort Mother's Line

King Bohemond III   King Ruben   King Hugh Lusignon   Count Baldwin
of Aquitaine   of Armenia -   of Cyprus   of Ibelin
      /   /   /   /

Prince Raymond **m** Princess Alice   King Amalric   **m**   Dame Eschiva
of Poitiers Antioch   of Armenia   of Jerusalem   of Ibelin
        /   /

Prince Raymond Roupen   **married**   Princess Heloise de Lusignon
of Antioch and Armenia   of Cyprus and Jerusalem
                      /

Marie St Gilles de Poitiers- Lusignon,- Ibelin, Princess of Armenia,Cyprus
and Jerusalem, Dame of Antioch and Tripoli

Married -Count Philippe de Montfort l'Amaury Lord of Tyre
                     /

Henri St Gilles de Montfort l'Amaury-Castres (The Lion)
Prince of Jerusalem, Armenia and Cyprus
Count of Tripoli, Toron, Tyre, Antioch and Beirut
Knight Commander of The Hospitaller Order of St John of Jerusalem

Married

Marquise Maria de Gothia

Abbess of The Order of The Knights of St Anthony the Hermit

About Kings Hart Books
Kings Hart Books is a small, independent publisher.

Our other fiction titles:
The Invisible Worm by Eileen O'Conor ISBN 978-1-906154-00-4
The Reso by Ambrose Conway (educational) ISBN 978-1-906154-01-1
Meeting Coty by Ruth Estevez ISBN 978-1906154-03-5
Apartment C by Ruth Learner ISBN 978-1-906-154-06-6
The Price by Tony Macnabb ISBN ISBN 978-1-906-154-08-0

Please visit our website at www.kingshart.co.uk for extracts and further
information.

Available to order at bookshops or through online retailer.

Printed in the United Kingdom
by Lightning Source UK Ltd.
135836UK00001B/403-447/P